D H
4—

D1621843

Danger in the Dark

SELECTED FICTION WORKS BY L. RON HUBBARD

FANTASY

The Case of the Friendly Corpse
Death's Deputy
Fear
The Ghoul
The Indigestible Triton
Slaves of Sleep & The Masters of Sleep
Typewriter in the Sky
The Ultimate Adventure

SCIENCE FICTION

Battlefield Earth
The Conquest of Space
The End Is Not Yet
Final Blackout
The Kilkenny Cats
The Kingslayer
The Mission Earth Dekalogy*
Ole Doc Methuselah
To the Stars

ADVENTURE

The Hell Job series

WESTERN

Buckskin Brigades
Empty Saddles
Guns of Mark Jardine
Hot Lead Payoff

A full list of L. Ron Hubbard's
novellas and short stories is provided at the back.

*Dekalogy—a group of ten volumes

L. RON HUBBARD

Danger
in the
Dark

GALAXY
PRESS

Published by
Galaxy Press, LLC
7051 Hollywood Boulevard, Suite 200
Hollywood, CA 90028

© 2008 L. Ron Hubbard Library. All Rights Reserved.

Any unauthorized copying, translation, duplication, importation or distribution,
in whole or in part, by any means, including electronic copying, storage or
transmission, is a violation of applicable laws.

Mission Earth is a trademark owned by L. Ron Hubbard Library and
is used with permission. *Battlefield Earth* is a trademark owned
by Author Services, Inc. and is used with permission.

Horsemen illustration from *Western Story Magazine* is © and ™ Condé Nast
Publications and is used with their permission. Cover art and story illustrations;
Fantasy, Far-Flung Adventure and Science Fiction illustrations; Story Preview and
Glossary illustrations and *A Matter of Matter* cover art: *Unknown* and *Astounding
Science Fiction* copyright © by Street & Smith Publications, Inc.
Reprinted with permission of Penny Publications, LLC.

Printed in the United States of America.

ISBN-10 1-59212-367-8
ISBN-13 978-1-59212-367-4

Library of Congress Control Number: 2007927517

Contents

Stories from Pulp Fiction's Golden Age

A ND it *was* a golden age.
The 1930s and 1940s were a vibrant, seminal time for a gigantic audience of eager readers, probably the largest per capita audience of readers in American history. The magazine racks were chock-full of publications with ragged trims, garish cover art, cheap brown pulp paper, low cover prices—and the most excitement you could hold in your hands.

"Pulp" magazines, named for their rough-cut, pulpwood paper, were a vehicle for more amazing tales than Scheherazade could have told in a million and one nights. Set apart from higher-class "slick" magazines, printed on fancy glossy paper with quality artwork and superior production values, the pulps were for the "rest of us," adventure story after adventure story for people who liked to *read*. Pulp fiction authors were no-holds-barred entertainers—real storytellers. They were more interested in a thrilling plot twist, a horrific villain or a white-knuckle adventure than they were in lavish prose or convoluted metaphors.

The sheer volume of tales released during this wondrous golden age remains unmatched in any other period of literary history—hundreds of thousands of published stories in over nine hundred different magazines. Some titles lasted only an issue or two; many magazines succumbed to paper shortages during World War II, while others endured for decades yet. Pulp fiction remains as a treasure trove of stories you can read, stories you can love, stories you can remember. The stories were driven by plot and character, with grand heroes, terrible villains, beautiful damsels (often in distress), diabolical plots, amazing places, breathless romances. The readers wanted to be taken beyond the mundane, to live adventures far removed from their ordinary lives—and the pulps rarely failed to deliver.

In that regard, pulp fiction stands in the tradition of all memorable literature. For as history has shown, good stories are much more than fancy prose. William Shakespeare, Charles Dickens, Jules Verne, Alexandre Dumas—many of the greatest literary figures wrote their fiction for the readers, not simply literary colleagues and academic admirers. And writers for pulp magazines were no exception. These publications reached an audience that dwarfed the circulations of today's short story magazines. Issues of the pulps were scooped up and read by over thirty million avid readers each month.

Because pulp fiction writers were often paid no more than a cent a word, they had to become prolific or starve. They also had to write aggressively. As Richard Kyle, publisher and editor of *Argosy*, the first and most long-lived of the pulps, so pointedly explained: "The pulp magazine writers, the best of them, worked for markets that did not write for critics or attempt to satisfy timid advertisers. Not having to answer to anyone other than their readers, they wrote about human beings on the edges of the unknown, in those new lands the future would explore. They wrote for what we would become, not for what we had already been."

Some of the more lasting names that graced the pulps include H. P. Lovecraft, Edgar Rice Burroughs, Robert E. Howard, Max Brand, Louis L'Amour, Elmore Leonard, Dashiell Hammett, Raymond Chandler, Erle Stanley Gardner, John D. MacDonald, Ray Bradbury, Isaac Asimov, Robert Heinlein—and, of course, L. Ron Hubbard.

In a word, he was among the most prolific and popular writers of the era. He was also the most enduring—hence this series—and certainly among the most legendary. It all began only months after he first tried his hand at fiction, with L. Ron Hubbard tales appearing in *Thrilling Adventures, Argosy, Five-Novels Monthly, Detective Fiction Weekly, Top-Notch, Texas Ranger, War Birds, Western Stories,* even *Romantic Range.* He could write on any subject, in any genre, from jungle explorers to deep-sea divers, from G-men and gangsters, cowboys and flying aces to mountain climbers, hard-boiled detectives and spies. But he really began to shine when he turned his talent to science fiction and fantasy of which he authored nearly fifty novels or novelettes to forever change the shape of those genres.

Following in the tradition of such famed authors as Herman Melville, Mark Twain, Jack London and Ernest Hemingway, Ron Hubbard actually lived adventures that his own characters would have admired—as an ethnologist among primitive tribes, as prospector and engineer in hostile climes, as a captain of vessels on four oceans. He even wrote a series of articles for *Argosy,* called "Hell Job," in which he lived and told of the most dangerous professions a man could put his hand to.

Finally, and just for good measure, he was also an accomplished photographer, artist, filmmaker, musician and educator. But he was first and foremost a *writer,* and that's the L. Ron Hubbard we come to know through the pages of this volume.

This library of Stories from the Golden Age presents the best of L. Ron Hubbard's fiction from the heyday of storytelling, the Golden Age of the pulp magazines. In these eighty volumes, readers are treated to a full banquet of 153 stories, a kaleidoscope of tales representing every imaginable genre: science fiction, fantasy, western, mystery, thriller, horror, even romance—action of all kinds and in all places.

Because the pulps themselves were printed on such inexpensive paper with high acid content, issues were not meant to endure. As the years go by, the original issues of every pulp from *Argosy* through *Zeppelin Stories* continue crumbling into brittle, brown dust. This library preserves the L. Ron Hubbard tales from that era, presented with a distinctive look that brings back the nostalgic flavor of those times.

L. Ron Hubbard's Stories from the Golden Age has something for every taste, every reader. These tales will return you to a time when fiction was good clean entertainment and the most fun a kid could have on a rainy afternoon or the best thing an adult could enjoy after a long day at work.

Pick up a volume, and remember what reading is supposed to be all about. Remember curling up with a *great story*.

—Kevin J. Anderson

KEVIN J. ANDERSON *is the author of more than ninety critically acclaimed works of speculative fiction, including* The Saga of Seven Suns, *the continuation of the* Dune Chronicles *with Brian Herbert, and his* New York Times *bestselling novelization of L. Ron Hubbard's* Ai! Pedrito!

Danger in the Dark

Danger in the Dark

BILLY NEWMAN looked wearily at the apathetic face and needed no fine physician to tell him that he gazed upon death. For all its flat nose and thick lips and narrow brow, it was—or had been—pleasant, always filled with happiness as only the face of the simple can be. Osea had been a good boy. He had trudged stoutheartedly after his fellah mahstah, carrying heavy loads through the thickest of jungle and the hottest of days, through the thundering rains and the parching droughts. Osea would trudge no more. His machete and the artistry with which he used it could avail him nothing now against this unseen enemy, the Red Plague.

Fifteen hundred miles to the north and west lay Manila; but no frail dugout prow could breast that distance, much less traverse it in time to bring relief to Kaisan Isle. Fifteen hundred miles away and no steamer would stop for another six months, and even if a lugger put in, the one word *smallpox* would drive the vessel seaward again as fast as the trade winds blow.

Osea was dying. Billy Newman sat beside the bunk and wondered how many hours or how many days would pass before the witch doctor would have to bury him—Osea and those others down in the village who were even now fighting with their last gasps to live.

Billy Newman had never before felt so lonely—and he had had aloneness as his constant companion, it seemed, for all his days. Futility weighed down upon his slender shoulders and bowed them. His small face, which tried to be stronger in its possession of a thin, silken mustache, showed how many hours it had been since last he had slept. The only thing he had to encourage him in this was that he himself had long ago been filled brimming with the antitoxin. Perhaps it was still strong enough to keep him from getting the disease. But he had no real concern for himself in any event. These people, already wasted by the ravages of Spain and the white man's unhealthy civilization, hardly deserved the gruesome tricks fate played upon them. And to think of their laughter being stilled forever was more than Billy Newman could bear.

He had no slightest inkling of the source of the disease. The last ship in had left six months before, and certainly it had had a clean bill of health. Kaisan, at the southern end of the Robber Islands, was too small to merit more than a yearly call of a small tramp. There was no reason for more. Kaisan, like ten thousand of its brothers, offered little or no inducement to trade. When it rained one swam rather than walked. And when the rains went away the land withered and parched. Copra, these last few years, had cost more to grow than its selling price, and of other crops, it raised none.

Billy wondered dully why he had ever come here. He knew but he had not energy enough just then to recall the answer. Through a lucky gold strike in Luzon he had amassed eight thousand dollars and—he had thought it was still good luck—he had been told that he could buy Kaisan for six thousand. He had bought.

Sitting there, waiting dispiritedly for Osea to die, he mulled over his arrival. At first he had laughed about it, not wishing to appear daunted by such nonsense. But now he well remembered what the fleeing seller had said.

The German had stood on the beach, eagerly watching his dunnage being loaded into a longboat. His fat, sun-fried face was filled with a glee which had long been foreign to it—but with a nervousness, too, as though he expected, even at this last instant, to be struck down where he stood.

"Goot-by, goot-by," he said for the hundredth time. "Py colly, Newman, I wish you all der luck I got—which ain't so much. But py damn, Newman, you vatch yourself, you hear? You look ouit. Don't pull no funny pizness. I got mein dollars, and now I don't vant to leave you mitout telling you to vatch it. Ven I get to Manila I von't say noddings. I von't breathe a void abouit it. I ain't no svindler. And ven I get around I vill tell dem for you that you'll take six t'ousand dollars for der place. Maybe next year, py colly, ven der steamer cooms, it brings a buyer. I'll do dot, Newman, I ain't no svindler."

"Maybe I won't want to sell," said Billy with a smile, surveying the white beach and the pleasant house and the native village and hearing the drums going to welcome him.

"Hah! Maybe you von't vant to sell. Captung, you listen at him."

"I heard him," said the ship captain, grinning. "But I hope I bring you a buyer when I come just the same. And, more'n that, 'cause I ain't so tough as I'm painted, I hope we'll find you alive."

"If you mean these people may turn on me—" began Billy.

"The people?" said the German. "No, py gott, dem fellers ain't goin' to hurt you none. Dem fellers is fine fellers, py colly."

"What is wrong, then?" persisted Billy.

"Vell . . ." the German looked searchingly at him. "No, py gott, you'll find it out for yourself. You von't pelief it anyvay even if I dell you."

"That's a comfort," said Billy. "If I won't believe it, maybe it isn't so."

"Oh, it's so, all right," said the captain. "At least Hans here is the first live and kicking white man we've pulled out of here in eight years—and that's how long I've been on this run. You'll find the rest of them over in the native cemetery with the gugus—and there are more dead natives around here than live ones by a hell of a ways. He means about Tadamona. That's what seems to get 'em."

"Who?"

"Tadamona. He's the boss spirit around here. About seventy-five feet tall. If you see him or displease him, he either makes the plague come or he blows the place around with a typhoon."

"Oh," said Billy, grinning broadly. "If I didn't know these islands better . . . Why, hell's bells, gentlemen, there isn't an island in the Pacific that hasn't its seventy-five-foot spirit. But I've never happened to meet one." He chuckled. "I thought you were talking about something real there for a while."

The captain and Hans had exchanged a glance and a shrug. They gravely took their final leave of him and then put off in the longboat to go geysering through the reef surf and out toward the steamer. By their heads Billy could see that they were talking dolorously about him. And there he had been left in a circle of baggage while the village chiefs in all their grass and feathers had marched down to acknowledge his leadership. He noted that they seemed to be in very good practice.

But still he was not going to be caught believing in such nonsense. The plague was the plague and nothing more. It had leaped, it was true, from nowhere, and before it would depart a good hundred of the two thousand would mark its path with white gravestones. Plague was plague. The villain was a small microbe, not a seventy-five-foot, wholly mythical god.

The medicine drums were beating wearily and another, greater drum had commenced to boom with a hysteria which spoke of breaking nerves. The slither and slap of bare feet sounded upon Billy's verandah, and he straightened up to see that Wanoa and several lesser chiefs had come.

They greeted him with deep bows, their faces stiff to hide the terror within them.

"*Hafa?*" said Billy, giving it the "What's the matter" intonation.

"We come to seek your help," said Wanoa.

"I have done all I can," replied Billy. "But if you think what little medicine I have may stave off any new case . . ." He got slowly to his feet and reached mechanically for his topee, although it was already night.

"Medicine does no good," said Wanoa with dignity. "We have found it necessary to use strong means—" He paused, cutting the flow of his Chamorro off short, as though he realized that what he was about to say would not go well with the mahstah.

"And?" said Billy, feeling it somehow.

"We turn back to old rite. Tonight we sacrifice young girl to Tadamona. Maybe it will be that he will turn away his anger—"

"A young girl?" gaped Billy. "You mean . . . you're going to kill—"

"We are sorry. It is necessary. Long time ago priests come. They tell us about fellah mahstah Jesus Christ. We say fine. Bime-by island got nothing but crosses. Tadamona is boss god Kaisan. Tadamona does not like to be forgotten. For a long time he slept. And then he see no sacrifices coming anymore. He get angry. For thirty years we get no rest. We get sick, all the best people die, the crops are bad, the typhoons throw our houses down. Then white men here get plenty power and Tadamona jealous and not like. Things get worse and worse. Tadamona no like white man because white man say he is boss. Tadamona is boss."

"You can't do this," said Billy quietly. "I won't let you murder—"

"We not murder anybody," said Wanoa. "Christina say she happy to die if people get saved."

"Christina! Why, she . . . she's a mission girl! You're lying! She's half-white! She would never consent to such a thing!"

Wanoa made a beckoning motion at the door, and Christina came shyly inside to stand with downcast face.

Billy walked toward her and placed his hand on her shoulder. Very often these last months he had watched her and wondered why he should go on forever alone. He would spend the rest of his life here, and Christina—she had that fragile beauty of the mestiza, beauty enough to turn the heads of most white men.

"You consented to this?" said Billy.

She nodded, not looking at him.

"Christina, you know something of white ways. You know what you have been taught. This Tadamona—why, he is nothing but airy mist. He is a superstition born out of typhoons and sickness and the minds of men who know little. Tadamona does not exist except in your imagination, and your death could do nothing to drive off this plague. You would only add another gravestone in the cemetery, and all the village would weep for you when the disease went on unabated." And as she did not seem to be listening, he raised his voice with sudden fury. "You fools! Your island god doesn't live! He never did live, and he never will! Give me this week and I'll stop this plague! Obey my orders and it will take no more of your people! Tadamona! Damn such a rotten idea!"

They stared at him with shocked attitudes, then glanced uneasily out into the darkness.

"You must not speak so," said Christina in a hushed voice. "He . . . he will come for you."

"How can he come for me if he doesn't exist?" cried Billy.

"You have seen the footprints in the rock," said Wanoa.

"A trick of lava!" shouted Billy. "No man or god has feet ten feet long!"

"You have heard him grumbling in the caverns of the point," said Wanoa.

"A trick of the sea in hollow coral!"

"You have seen where he has torn up palms by the roots," persisted Wanoa.

"They were ready to fall at the slightest breeze. I tell you, you can't do this! Tadamona is in your heads, and only in your heads, do you understand? If he lives, why haven't I seen him? Why?"

"He is too cunning for that," said Wanoa. "And to see him, to look him full in the face, is to die. Those of our people who have seen him have been found dead, unmarked, in the streets. The wise ones here never stir about after midnight."

"Bah! If he exists let him come and show himself to me! Let him walk up that path and call on me!"

They shrank back away from him as though expecting him to fall dead on the instant. Even Christina moved until his hand fell from her arm.

He was tired again. He felt so very alone and so small. "You can't do this, Christina. Give me a week and I'll stop this plague. I promise it. If I do not, then do what you like. But give me that."

"More people will die," said Christina. "I am not afraid."

"It is the white blood in her," said Wanoa. "It will quiet Tadamona. In a week, we will lose many, many more."

Billy walked up and down the grass mat for minutes. He was weary unto death himself, and these insistent voices bored like awls into his skull. Again he flared:

"So a week is too much to give me?"

"You have had a week," said Wanoa impassively.

Billy faced them, his small face flushed under the flickering hurricane lantern, the wind from the sea stirring his silky blond hair. For the moment he filled his narrow jacket completely. "Yes, damn you, I've had a week! A week obstructed by your yap-yap-yap about Tadamona. If a week is too much, how many days?"

"One day," said Wanoa. "Not many people die in one day."

"One day?" cried Billy. "What— All right," he said, jacket emptying again. "One day. And when that is through I suppose . . ." He glanced at Christina and saw that she would hold to her word then.

Wanoa made a motion for the others to leave, and then he walked slowly after them down the path to the beach. Once Christina stopped and glanced toward the house, and Billy, seeing her, looked up into the sky as though help could be found there.

"One day," he muttered to himself. "A lot of chance I have to stop that in one day. They're fools. They're all fools. Tadamona! By God, if I could get my hands on him once . . ." And then, stumbling toward his bedroom, he stopped and laughed shakily. "If I don't watch myself, I'll be believing it too."

Osea, seeing and hearing nothing, lay on the couch. Billy covered him against the evening chill and then, finding no reason to maintain his vigil, dropped under the mosquito netting of his own bunk fully clothed. Presently he slept.

Tadamona, God of Jungle. Ageless as thought itself. Tadamona, seventy-five feet from toe to crown, with the face of a shark and the deadliness of the barracuda. Tadamona, childishly simple and childishly cruel. Jealous he had once been even of his own son and before such wrath the son had fled, leaving Tadamona to bring ill luck to Kaisan in all his lonely majesty. Tadamona had left his footprints in cold lava that men might see his size. Great five-toed prints, measuring ten feet, having every swirl and arch. One gazed upon Tadamona and sickened and died. One forgot to placate him and the typhoons came. One neglected to offer him fish and the next time at sea the banca sank, its owner never to be seen again.

And out on the long point, whose sheer cliffs disdainfully reared high above the long Pacific swell, there was a monstrous cave, a full hundred feet from floor to roof, a thousand feet from entrance to entrance. Men said it was there. No man had courage enough to make certain.

Tadamona, the awful and fearsome god of Kaisan, walked beside the sea that night, dwarfing the royal palms at his sides, stepping on and crushing native bancas, too small to be noticed.

And Billy Newman slept uneasily and dreamed awful things, hearing in the deepest of his slumber the hoarse breathing of Osea, the boy who would no longer trot so happily upon his fellah mahstah's heels.

The moon had ridden down the sky, masked by the frightened clouds which fitfully blocked its light. The palm fronds rattled together like old bones in a weird, unholy dance. The shifting shadow patterns changed upon the verandah. Billy Newman stirred restively.

He did not know what woke him. But he was awake and one hand was clutched around the clammy butt of his automatic and his gaze was riveted upon the window, seen thinly through the mosquito netting.

He waited, hardly daring to breathe. He could see nothing—yet. He could hear nothing—yet. But he knew, without knowing how he knew, that something moved out there in the moonlight—something ominous and horrible.

At last he saw a shadow sweep across his floor. He tightened his grip on the gun. The shadow was as tall as a man and it moved without the slightest sound. Billy raised his gun, feverishly telling himself that this was some vengeful Chamorro come to settle a fancied score.

The mosquito net quivered uncertainly, plucked by a fumbling hand. Billy, inside the glowing white of it, felt as though he lay in his coffin.

The end of the net raised slowly, still uncertainly, as an elephant might push it out of the way with his trunk. The shadow Billy Newman had seen was now over him, too high over him to be a man. And now thick stumps like fingers, each one as tall as a man in itself, slid under the net and groped. Billy recoiled from the chill touch, as though they were snakes. The movement brought him to himself. The automatic in his hand he jammed straight into the horny flesh. With the rapidity of hysteria he pulled the trigger and seven thundering flashes lit the room.

He could hear nothing—yet. But he knew, without knowing how he knew, that something moved out there in the moonlight—something ominous and horrible.

The hand flinched a very little and then, with savage, crushing strength, fastened upon Billy. The net was ripped away. The hand withdrew, banging Billy against the sill.

His staring eyes took in a horrible sight. A grotesque face with seven rows of teeth hovered over him, weirdly haloed by the moon. The thing got to its feet, crushing down a royal palm. Billy, inverted, stared at the earth far below, at his house which was suddenly so small.

The thing marched soundlessly down the beach, heading for the point which went out to meet the sea.

The world began to spin for Billy. He was quivering and sick, overcome by the awful stench of this thing and by the height and the doubt as to his fate. The automatic spun around his nerveless finger and dropped down to the beach. The last thing his eyes saw, as they rolled sickly into his head, was the thing sucking upon its injured finger, much as a man removes small splinters from his flesh.

After that Billy closed his eyes and fought the terror which surged up to engulf his reason. He knew now why men died when they saw this thing. It would be so easy to lie inert and let his own life ebb. It would be a relief to die.

Minutes later, the shock of a short fall brought him to himself. He crouched instantly, staring about him, conscious, at first, only of shadowy shapes which loomed in a crimson haze. Then his glance rose, up and up, and he again found Tadamona, seated down upon a giant boulder and backed by the soaring height of the cavern. The rows of teeth in that shark face gleamed redly in the eerie light, and the hands upheld the head in an attitude of consideration.

15

Billy flashed his glance around the place to discover an exit. There were two, but long before he could hope to reach them this thing would stop him. He sank back, only to tense again on the discovery that he was thirty feet from the floor, precariously perched on a narrow ledge of coral.

A low, muttering sound came to him and mystified him until he reasoned that it was the surf beating through the hollow point. A smell of decay saturated the air about him and he traced it to piles of fish bones scattered all around.

He peered down and, then, between the thing's huge feet, he found the source of the light, a glowing, bubbling pool of molten stuff which sent up sulfurous vapors to wreathe the awful shape.

Tadamona was studying him. The lidless eyes were filled more with curiosity than anything else, but the glance could have been likened to the gaze of a beast interested in its soon-to-be-devoured prey.

It had not occurred to Billy that this thing might be able to speak, and when it did he was so startled that it took seconds for the gist of the words to sink through his terror.

"You are the white fellah mahstah," said Tadamona, his voice making the cave shiver in echo. His words were ancient Chamorro and Billy understood them well.

"You are the white fellah mahstah," repeated Tadamona. "Tonight, I am told, you said that you did not believe in god or devil. Tonight, they say, you sent word for me to come if I lived at all. Tonight, they say, you boasted that you were greater than all old gods."

Billy was fighting for calmness.

"You say you stop the sickness," continued Tadamona. "Perhaps you can also stop the storms, cast down the forests and raise them anew. But I see no great man. I see a weak fellah mahstah no bigger than a child. I see a man full of empty boasting and no reverence for the old gods."

"What are you . . . going to do with me?" said Billy.

"It is that I am thinking about," replied Tadamona. "You must be quiet." Again he clasped his chin in a mammoth hand and regarded his game. Thought was so foreign to that sluggish brain that one could almost see the slow chain of reason progress.

At last he said, "I am going to kill you. You have said that you have power greater than mine. If you have such power, you would have shown it before now, therefore you lie. You have boasted and your boasts are all lies and so I am going to kill you."

Billy tried to buck up. "You are going to kill me because you are afraid of me."

The effect was sudden and savage. Tadamona almost shook down the cave with his thunder. "Afraid? Afraid of you—more of a child than a man? *Afraid?*" And then his rage went swiftly into laughter and again the cave rocked as he sent forth peal after peal, holding his quaking sides. Finally he again grew calm. The laugh had been humorless for all the display, and the sound of it had driven Billy into dull fury.

"I am afraid of you?" said Tadamona. "I, who have ruled jungle and sea for as many years as the world is old? You come, you say you are a god, you say you can stop my sicknesses in one day. . . . You have lied and so you will die—"

"I tell you," howled Billy, "you are afraid. If you thought me less dangerous, you would not bother with me. When the people know that you took me and killed me, they will know, too, that you did it out of jealousy and fear. I have told them that I would stop the sickness—"

"An empty boast, white fool. You are weak. You are nothing."

"I am strong enough to make you afraid. *You* are the coward. Where is your power over sickness? You have none. Where is your power over storm? That, too, is a lie. You are the liar and the boaster, not I. Else you would not have to kill me to show your superiority over me!"

Billy was beginning to gather his wits. It mattered little what he did or said. He could make his own position no worse. "Already you understand that you lie," he cried into the thing's face. "The Chamorro, when he sees you, falls down in death. I am still alive. Only looking on you can never kill me. My medicine and my magic are stronger than yours."

Tadamona again stared thoughtfully at him, and then reached out a tree trunk of a finger and stirred him up experimentally, almost knocking him from the ledge. The effort Billy made to keep his hold amused the brute and put him into a better frame of mind.

"You have greater magic than mine," he mocked. "You shriek in terror that I am afraid of you. You are funny. The people think you are a great man. You have told them that you are greater than I am. Very well, white fellah mahstah, there you see the entrance to this place. You will go. You will return to the house from which I took you. Shortly I shall bring my sickness. I shall bring my storm. When I have

18

finished, neither man nor tree shall stand aright upon this island. Nothing will live. And before they die, they will know that you lied. Go."

Billy stood in astonishment.

"Go!" said Tadamona insistently. "Tomorrow we shall match our magic. And I shall prove to you before you die how much you have lied."

Billy waited for no more urging. He scrambled down off the ledge and sprinted for the entrance to the cavern, and as he dashed through and up the great passageway which led to the air he could hear Tadamona laughing, like a typhoon in the palms behind him. And the relief at being free was completely engulfed in the despair at his own helplessness.

The pale face of the moon was frightened behind the swift sweep of racing clouds. Shadows restively leaped into being and vanished along the rough trail, making the overwrought Billy feel that a thousand smaller demons lay in ambush at every turn. But when he had reached the whitely paved cart road which ended at his bungalow, the lessened strain gave him a moment's clear thought, and he realized, with the suddenness of a bullet, that he had sold out the entire island for the sake of a few more hours of life. He had bought his momentary respite in terrible coin and unless he found that thousandth chance to avert this disaster, the lives of all were upon his head. He alone had goaded Tadamona into such vengeful folly.

Exhausted and shaking, he reached his verandah and fumbled his way through the dark front room to find a light for the lamp. The leaping yellow flame gave him spirit and returned courage. He even laughed a little and then checked it for fear it was hysteria in borning.

This was all, clearly, the most exquisite madness that could happen to a man. And before five minutes had passed, Billy Newman walked around the table and threw himself in a chair and said aloud, "What a silly dream that was."

And, for the moment, it seemed very like a dream. He could almost recall waking up and walking in here for a calming cigarette. Nerves made nightmares and that was all there was to it. He poured himself a small drink, saying that he would take it off and then return to bed and calmer sleep. But with the glass halfway to his lips, it occurred to him that he should look in upon Osea. Maybe the boy would come out of the coma after all.

He got up and walked back to his bedroom, picking up the lamp on his way. The leaping light played for a moment on the awful face of the boy. No, Osea was still on the threshold of death, beyond any help but God's. Billy lowered the lamp, feeling very tired. The dream had not changed poor Osea's condition.

Billy returned to the living room, so deep in sadness that he failed to realize that there was now no wind in the palms outside. He did not discover the lack for several minutes and when he did, he gave a start as though someone had made a great noise.

No wind. That was strange. At this time of year that wind never failed. And for months the clatter of fronds had been a ceaseless undertone to everything heard. It was so incredible that he went out on the verandah to find out whether he had suddenly become deaf. But no, the fronds hung in limp despair but dimly seen in moonlight which was now yellow and somehow oppressive. It was hot, too. So hot that Billy's small mustache was thick with sweat, and his shirt was glued to his skin.

He started back into the house when the glint of a glass stopped him. He raised the lamp to look at the face of his barometer. Three times he looked away and looked back again to make certain he was seeing right. But in the last few minutes, the needle had fallen *from thirty to twenty-seven and was still going down.* Anxiously he stared at the small notches which were marked "Typhoon."

A horrible suffocation took hold of him. He whirled and raced down the steps to stop, holding the lamp high over his head. The pale glow extended just far enough for him to see the great footprints on the beach—footprints ten feet long!

He had caught at a straw. He had made-believe it was a dream in the hope of brushing it all away. But here were the prints, there was the glass. Already Tadamona's awful power had reached out to engulf the island.

Billy felt as though something was about to snap in his mind. Up until now, even when in the presence of the thing, he had half believed it to be a nightmare. But now he was awake and the entire thing was so.

He would get help. He would rouse the village. He would make them fight and destroy Tadamona forever. Somehow he would have to overcome their terror—for if he did not, dawn would find not a living soul on Kaisan.

He fled through the palms toward the village, and as he

drew near the shadowy shapes of the thatched huts, he could hear restlessness and moaning. The largest one, in the center of the village, formerly the long house and once a Christian church, was now the home of Wanoa. And Billy was convinced that once Wanoa, that sturdy warrior, completely understood that it was either death by storm and plague or death in battle, he would certainly choose the latter.

Billy hammered loudly upon the door and all within went silent. When nobody came, he shouted, "Open up! It's your fellah mahstah!"

Wanoa's impassive face showed in a dark rectangle of window which was cautiously opened. Wanoa studied his visitor for some time before he consented to unbolt the door.

Billy burst into the bare-floored room, still holding his lamp. It was in his throat to shout out his news, but the sight he saw there stopped him. Five people—all the members of the chief's household—lay along the far wall. A few hours before only one had been ill, but now all five were ashen!

"What is this?" cried Billy.

Wanoa's tone was hostile. "Tonight you say you stop sickness. Tonight you forbid sacrifice to Tadamona. And now all but maybe ten in whole village sick. You have spoken evilly. The god is punishing us all."

Billy, still on the verge of stating his business, felt a clammy terror, held by the rest of them, enter into himself. He heard a sudden movement at the door and was so on edge that he whirled and almost spilled his lamp.

It was Christina, who had seen his coming. Gone was the

shy, delicate beauty Billy had always known. Her eyes blazed with hatred and the scorn in her voice was like thrown acid.

"*You* forbade the rites! *You* have caused this to come. And now the sea lies motionless and waiting. The wind has stopped. The village is dying, and only a fool would not know that a typhoon is at hand. This is the end of Kaisan and you, wretched white man, have caused its downfall!"

It was so true that Billy had no answer. He stared at Christina, half of him detached and astonished at the unmasked savagery in the woman, at the strength of which he did not at all disapprove.

"You are right," he said in a low voice. "I have caused this, but now I have come for help. I have seen the god"—there was a sharp intake of breath and all eyes, the many which now peered in at the door, grew wide upon him—"I have seen the god and I know where he is to be found. With enough men it may be possible to kill him—"

"You have seen him and are alive?" said Wanoa.

"With enough men!" mocked Christina. "All the men of the island, armed as your white soldiers are armed, could not even injure Tadamona. But we have no arms and our men are all ill. Because of you, we shall die!"

Billy saw that she struck the pitch for the others. He saw men in the door with hard hands on their machetes. It would take but very little to rouse them to murder him.

"I understand that now," said Billy. "I did not think. My mind was frozen. But now I have a plan. If only a few will help me, we may yet save this place from destruction."

23

His words fell into the ominous silence which waited for the storm. Nervously he spoke again. "In an outhouse near my bungalow is stored the dynamite we have used for clearing. There are a dozen cases still left. The point where the thing lives is hollow from the wear of the sea, and the shore end of it shows evidence of connection with Mount Kinea above. With help I can place the dynamite on the shore end and set it off. There is enough to break through the crust and perhaps cause the lava pools to explode. It is true that everyone will die before dawn. But isn't it better to die trying, than like whimpering women in these huts?"

"It cannot succeed!" said Christina. "I know nothing of your dynamite, but I have seen the power of Tadamona. You can avail nothing against it."

"I can try," said Billy.

"And we can refuse," said Christina. "The few who are left may live even yet. The sick are too weak to help. Go back to your bungalow and dwell upon the calamity which you have brought to us."

It was well that she said he was to go. The men at the door fell away to let him pass when, just as swiftly, they would have cut him down.

He paused, looking back at her, the light of his lantern making her smooth, satin skin glow with an almost luminous light. "Whether I have help or not, I must try. There is but little time left." He faced about and strode down the lane between the huts and back through the jungle which opened out again upon his bungalow.

The futility of the gesture he planned lay like lead in his heart, but he could not stand inactivity. He went to the hut which housed the machinery of the island, and climbed up into the ancient, tanklike truck which had seen a dozen years of service before it had ever rolled a wheel on Kaisan. It started reluctantly, and he eased it out and around to the roadway which led to the powder shack.

He left the engine running and unlocked the door. He was too discouraged to be careful and set his lamp where it would shed the best light. He counted the cases and found that he had three more than he had thought. But still, it was little enough for a job at which howitzers themselves might have failed.

The electric blasting machine was rusty and damp, and the handle was difficult to pull up. He took it out into the moonlight and, after exerting much force, was able to raise it. He thrust it down again, watching for the end wires to spark. It required several tries before he at last saw their feeble flicker. It was inviting a misfire to use it at all, but all his caps were electric and of the kind used in damp metal mines. He put the machine in the truck and returned to begin on the dynamite.

He had carried about half the boxes outside when his eye was arrested by another type of container, and he stopped to pick it up. Against the chance that the tramp steamer might sometime be forced to unload at night, a long-dead owner had purchased a gross of magnesium flares. Billy put several inside his shirt. For lack of other firing equipment he might find a way to press them into service, as their ignition caps might serve where the electric machine failed.

He picked up another case and carried it outside. Startled by a movement beside the truck, he stopped. And then, with relief, he saw that it was Christina.

She had shed the prosaic mission costume that her movements might be freer, replacing it with a sarong which closely molded her beautiful form. The eerie character of the moonlight gave her the appearance of a jungle cat.

"You had better go back to your hut," said Billy.

"Save your breath for work. It is barely possible that your plan may work."

He turned and pulled the rest of the dynamite from the shack, and then helped her fling it up into the body of the truck. He made it fast with some old pieces of hemp, and then they climbed up to the seat. He eased the truck down the jungle-bordered trail. Its lights did not seem to have the power to penetrate this thickening, suffocating murk.

"It may stop him for a little while," said Christina. "If we are alive at dawn, we will have another day."

"How do you know that?"

"He has never been known to walk by day."

Billy looked up at the moon. Although there were no clouds, it was now almost hidden. The heat was so thick he found it very difficult to breathe after his exertions.

"This is all crazy mad," he said abruptly. "But when I tried to tell myself it was a dream, I found a barometer and his footprints and knew that I had really seen him. Sickness is caused by bacteria, and typhoons are too great a difference in high and low pressure areas. But it is impossible for all the village to become ill at once, and equally impossible for the storm to come on so suddenly."

"You are through laughing at us, then?"

"I have never laughed at you."

"The people believe something else. They know white men think they are gods, though they act as the lowest of men."

"I don't feel anything near a god right now," said Billy with a feeble attempt at a smile.

They drove up the cart road, and it was as though they forced against a wall of sinuous substance which was reluctant to let them through.

"There is the point," he said at last.

She gazed at it without flinching. "You saw him and still live?"

"I saw him."

"Then perhaps I too can look upon him."

"Perhaps."

"Maybe he is not there."

"Maybe."

They forced the truck up the strangely bare jungle path, where no native feet ever trod. It labored on the ascent and then, caught at last by heavy vines, stopped.

"There is a cavern just ahead. I saw it as I came out of its cave."

"I see it," she said, walking in front and peering into the murk. She looked at the darker hole beyond and knew it for what it was. She came back to Billy and helped him with the boxes.

Methodically they carried them to the cavern and lowered them down. One by one they placed and packed them, working with a slowness which was defiance in itself.

When they had done, they felt a stir in the air.

"The wind will be here in a moment," said Christina.

"Yes, I hear it."

He went back to the truck and took out the firing cable and the machine. He fitted caps into the sticks of the topmost box and then affixed the wire. He went back toward the truck and then beyond, letting out coil after coil. Finally he knelt and connected the blasting machine.

With Christina's help he piled stones and earth on top of the boxes. They were very quiet, unable to keep from watching the mouth of the cavern so short a distance from them.

Christina followed him back to the machine. The calm which she had so laboriously preserved was now beginning to crack.

"He has not come out. Perhaps he is not there at all!"

Billy again inspected his wires, saying nothing. The next instant, anything he might have said would have gone unheard. With a blast fully as loud as any dynamite explosion, the hurricane struck Kaisan. A torrent of stinging rain, lashed by the scream of the wind, battered them and blinded them. With a deafening thunder the sea rose up and crashed down upon the reef, snarling forward in its eagerness to claw the beaches.

Speech was impossible even at the distance of a foot. They

gripped the earth, stunned by the ferocity of the attack, chilled by wave after wave of rain, each one of which left them half drowned. Not ten feet from them a giant royal palm vanished to leave a dark cavern of its own. The very stones streaked away from the path. The wind was full of pelting sticks and leaves and fronds which left their bodies numb as from a flogging.

For ten minutes or more the first attack of the typhoon continued. Then there came a momentary lull as though the great beast paused to take a proud surveyal of what he had done and then blast away again at the most stubborn centers of resistance.

In the instant of respite, Billy groped for Christina and found her shivering at his side. All the while she had been clinging hard to his shoulder but that force was so small he had not felt it in the shock of wind and rain.

"There'll be nothing left of the island!" she wailed into his ear. "Blow up this place while we still have the calm!"

Billy got to his knees and placed both hands upon the handle. He thrust down with all his might. The ancient magneto whirred, the end of the plunger clanged against the breaker. Nothing happened. Billy fought the thing up again.

With redoubled fury the storm struck anew. He was torn from his grip on the handle and flung back against the earth. Dimly he saw Christina crawling toward him. She helped him breast the blast which swept up from the sea.

He braced himself and took the grips. Again he slammed the bar down.

In the countershock which followed, he lost Christina. The concussion sucked all the wind away for an instant and then the storm, angered, came howling back to pound him into the earth for such insolence. The explosion had been dull in the bedlam already loose, but through the medium of the ground, Billy felt a series of shakes and knew with a surge of triumph that the cavern was caving in.

Again the storm paused to draw its breath and Billy, feeling movement behind him, faced about as he hugged the earth to find Christina.

But it was not Christina. The thing went up like a tower into the sky. Billy sat back, staring upward and still upward, following the bulk of the two planted legs. He felt rather than saw the two gleaming eyes and the glistening rows of teeth.

"Tadamona!" he said, sickly.

The beast god grinned. The gale was hushed while he spoke. "You have the greater magic. You have stopped the people from dying, you have quelled the typhoon." The laughter rang from island peak to the sea and back again. "You have dropped the roof of a cavern, puny liar, and that is all. Look at your island! Remember how you found your people. It is an hour until dawn and in that hour Kaisan's pygmy men will end their days. But you are not to watch their going. See, feel proud! I halt the storm for the instant it will take to break you in half and cast you into the sea."

Tadamona stooped down and the engulfing shadow of his hand darkened the earth about Billy. He scrambled back, leaping to his feet in a wild attempt to flee from the outstretched fingers. Ahead there was only the cavern and that was now filled with rubble. There was no escape and Tadamona again sent the earth and sky rocking with his laughter to see such a vain struggle.

At the cavern, a few feet inside, Billy found a dead end. He whirled about and suddenly the terror gave way to fury. He was suddenly released from the paralysis which had first been his at the sight of the monster and now he cried out insane, incoherent phrases at the advancing thing.

Tadamona knelt, crouching like a cat about to flick a mouse out of its hole. The clawed fingers drew close to Billy. Savagely he kicked at them, insensible to the pain he caused his own foot. Tadamona, unable to get a sure grip, knelt lower and peered closely with his luminous eyes.

Billy leaped behind a small pile of rocks, but the fingers only brushed them to one side as though they had been sand. With a final shriek of rage, Billy reached into his shirt and yanked out the until-now-forgotten magnesium flares. He bit off a cap with his teeth and hurled it at the face. The flare sparked and then blazed into brilliant white light.

Tadamona recoiled for an instant and then, with a horrifying fury of his own, snatched at and captured Billy, hauling him forth. Billy had another flare, and it, too, he ignited and threw straight at the eyes of the thing.

Billy felt himself jerk high into the air and knew that he had been thrown. He saw the dark earth and the darker jungle god all mingled with the sky. And then he landed in a tangle of vines, and the world went black and sick. But he was too conscious of hovering death to succumb to senselessness. He reeled to his feet and, with every ounce of willpower, followed through his last intention. With a rapidity of which he himself was not immediately conscious, he threw all the remaining flares at the gigantic bulk which had begun to grope anew for him.

One after the other the brilliant lights arced through the murk. There was an odor of singed hair in the wind. One after another the flares struck the path to send out their blinding glares which mounted in intensity as they burned.

Suddenly Tadamona was no longer searching for his quarry. With insane fury, holding both arms before his face, he was stamping at the flares. But their heat was too great for even his thick hide to stand, and he staggered back, blind in the light, howling in agony.

The savage whiteness of the light bathed the monster's entire hulk, lighting up the gleaming rows of teeth in the half-moon mouth, dragging out an agonized blaze from the awful eyes, glittering on the claws of hand and foot alike.

Billy stopped in amazement. He had hardly been conscious of his own actions. He had used the flares as the last, hopeless resort. But now a horrible thing was happening.

The thing seemed to melt. First there were no arms and then there was no face. The body became transparent to the moonlight which pierced the storm clouds and then, as Billy stared, the body was not there at all.

Far off, rising upward toward the overcast sky and dwindling there to nothing, a shriek went, went and vanished and was not heard again.

Billy was suddenly weak. He staggered out upon the path, floundering in the loose dust cast up by the explosion of his dynamite. One last flare burned and by its light he saw the two last prints of the giant, large and clear in the sand. He stared up from them, expecting to find the god still. But the sky was empty. The sky was empty and the moon was again showing through the tumbled clouds which fled into the west.

Alone, he staggered down the trail. He passed his truck and walked on, well knowing himself to be too shaky to drive it. He reached the white cart road and floundered along it, dully hoping that Christina had fled to safety.

His bungalow had lights in it, but he did not comment upon it—he was still so dazed. He went up the walk and across the verandah and stopped, holding himself up with the door.

A boy was there, bustling about and very worried. The boy's face was perfectly clear. At a slight sound Billy made, Osea turned anxiously and then relief flooded his face.

"Mahstah! You b'long doctah house. How come walk about this time?"

Billy ran an exploratory hand over Osea's young face. There was no mark or abrasion upon it. He sank into a chair, and Osea pressed a glass of brandy upon him which he drank mechanically.

How long he sat there he was not sure, but when he looked up it was daylight.

It was daylight and Wanoa was respectfully waiting with his retinue upon the verandah.

"Well?" said Billy.

Wanoa looked uneasy. He cleared his throat and straightened himself until he was as tall as possible. "We come to see how you like new work schedule. We got plenty men now. Nobody sick on whole island. You say work-work and we work. You no make much pay, we not make much pay. You say do, we do. You say want, you get." It was evidently not the speech which he had rehearsed with flowery gestures and effusive thanks. That speech was in his bearing and his face, but he was entirely too awed to voice it.

Billy nodded and the group withdrew to silently walk away from the house. But when they got to the beach, they suddenly raised their voices in joyful discourse and capered along as though they had been the children of the village instead of its most sacred elders.

Billy smiled and found that he felt amazingly good. He had just started to rise when he heard a thump just inside the door. He beheld Christina. She gave her bundle of belongings a further push with her foot, and then glared indignation at the astonished Osea.

"Go fix the fellah mahstah's bed before you get what for!" she cried. "And you. What are you doing still up? You need sleep. Much sleep."

She walked swiftly through the room and into the kitchen where Billy presently heard her abusing the cook for not having a better breakfast.

"Bah, you are a fool!" Christina cried at the luckless chef. "You think just because he is a god, he doesn't have to eat?"

Billy gazed self-consciously at his worn shoes and then up to find Osea staring at him. Osea grinned suddenly and Billy, stretching comfortably, grinned back.

The Room

The Room

UNCLE TOBY disappeared.

He had gone into his room one evening and hadn't been seen after that by anyone, not even Gracie, his horse.

Aunt Cinthia was bustling about the huge farm kitchen, doing the wrong thing with the wrong pans and pausing every few seconds to wipe "the steam" out of her eyes and vigorously blow her red nose upon her apron. She was a gigantic woman and her heart was huge in proportion, but her feet got in each other's way and her hands were so strong that they sometimes crumpled up china at a touch. Before Uncle Toby had married her she had been worked like a draft animal on her brother's farm. Her brother was a first-generation American and saw nothing wrong with making a woman plow if the horses needed saving.

"It's not like him!" said Aunt Cinthia, honking vigorously into her apron. "It ain't right for him to stay away so long. A week or ten days, that's maybe all right. But it's sixteen days and four hours! Joe, you don't . . . don't suppose something got him, do you? Some varmint, maybe?"

Joe shifted restively and knocked down his crutch. He was a quiet, usually cheerful boy and to see his "aunt" in such agony of suffering cut his nerves into little slivers. Joe had never seen Aunt Cinthia so upset and it had been brought home to him in the last few days just how deeply this tall, clumsy woman loved Uncle Toby. Ever since he was three Joe had been living with them, himself an orphan after a prairie fire got his parents, and he could not recall either of them ever showing any great affection. They never rowed together and they never said sweet things, either. They were just sort of—well—comfortable.

Uncle Toby, of course, was a very brainy man. He had studied at the State university, had graduated high as a veterinary and was forever reading books on all sorts of subjects. Naturally, Aunt Cinthia, who couldn't read, had no truck with books and so had little conversationally in common with Uncle Toby. Uncle Toby had rescued her, he had cared for her, he was her mainstay, her world, her idol. She never said anything about it. Sometimes her eyes had said things when Uncle Toby wasn't looking. But the way she was broken by this circumstance unnerved Joe.

Joe, well as he was able, had been out and around looking casually. It was hard for him to cover much territory for there wasn't much of his right leg and twenty-three years had not hung much fat on him. Pallid to transparency, frail and wistful and quiet, Joe had been too shy to ask the sheriff to let him join in the general hunt. Joe had poked into a few culverts and looked in a few bushes and had ridden Uncle Toby's mare, Gracie, all the way over to the hill. But he hadn't found any sign of Uncle Toby.

The sheriff hadn't found any sign, either. Neither had the other farmers and villagers. They all had liked Uncle Toby. He had taken care of their stock and, often, their children and

wives and it simply wasn't reasonable that Uncle Toby and
Palmerville could run separately.

The circumstances had been mysterious. About nine,
sixteen days before, with the summer twilight fading out,
Uncle Toby had come in the house. He had refused a cup
of coffee and had gone straight to his room. He had shut
the door as he always did. The next morning the door to the
room was still shut. But Uncle Toby had not been in there.
However, Joe and Aunt Cinthia had not found out about that
for three days.

This room of Uncle Toby's was an inviolable sanctuary.
The bushy-headed old man would often stay in there reading
for two days at a stretch, living either on nothing or on some
of the canned goods he always kept in a cupboard. That was
a clear and usual thing in this old farmhouse and nobody
thought there was anything strange in it, it had been going
on for so long.

Once Aunt Cinthia had thought she had heard some loud
voices in that room, but just Uncle Toby came out and she
forgot about it, not being a curious sort of person.

The room opened off the parlor. The old house had grown
up from a sod hut and had been added to as the years had gone
along until it was a pile of rooms. No architect could have
mapped from the outside just how Uncle Toby's room fitted
into the scheme. But it was there, in defiance of architecture.

It was never cleaned. When she had first come to this place,
Aunt Cinthia had started to clean it and in a very quiet voice
Uncle Toby had told her not to touch it again ever. And so
she had never touched it again ever. There was a potbellied

stove in the middle of it, a sandbox muchly missed beside the stove. There was a long rack full of medical books and another case full of other kinds of books. There was a big roll-top desk, but the cover had not been down for years, because there were too many papers on it to let the cover close. There were some pictures on the walls too thickly cased in dust to be recognized and there were some knick-knacks sitting on a side table and in a cabinet. There was a case of instruments and a mysterious black box which contained something electrical to accomplish something medical. The carpet was either red or green; the fact was uncertain.

Uncle Toby had not been seen coming out of his room. Gracie, the mare, was still in her stall. Nobody had phoned. And the fairs wouldn't begin for another month. Uncle Toby had just plain disappeared.

Sometimes he had taken trips which had begun with a call. He would go doctor somebody's pigs and the somebody would be going over to see somebody else and Uncle Toby would go along and spend the night and then go see somebody else and after having toured the whole country and having seen nearly everyone in it he would come home, ten days late, hang up his hat, put away his instrument case and wash his hands for supper just as though he had left that morning.

But Uncle Toby hadn't taken Gracie and Uncle Toby hated to walk. Nobody had been visited by him. He had simply vanished, leaving a hole in Palmerville which nobody else could ever begin to fill. Uncle Toby's white, bushy head and his warm, blue eyes didn't turn up this time.

Jeb, the hired man, came in to supper and the three sat

down in the kitchen and ate. There were towers of food. There was little eaten. Jeb didn't even clean his plate.

"What do you think, Jeb?" pleaded Aunt Cinthia.

Jeb judicially picked his teeth and gazed with washed-out eyes at the beam ceiling. He shook his head.

"Do you think he drowned, maybe?" said Aunt Cinthia.

Jeb shook his head again. He started to say something, then paused. He picked at a scrap of meat that was wedged in his spraddled teeth. He recrossed his legs. He shook his head again. After a little the strain got too great and he leaped up, jammed on his hat and stomped outside. There was a clang as he kicked a milk bucket off the back porch.

"I looked all over—far as I could," said Joe.

"Yes, Joe. I know you did," said Aunt Cinthia.

"I would have looked a lot farther only . . ." He glanced at his crutch with a scowl.

"You did all right, Joe."

"I . . . I didn't do enough," said Joe.

"There, there, Joe. Now don't you go breaking down. I'm a woman. I got a right to. But don't you. Joe . . ."

"Yes, Aunt Cinthia?"

"Joe, we got to admit it. I had a horrible dream. I am ashamed to think it, but I had a terrible nightmare. I got to admit it, Joe. We . . . we won't see Uncle Toby again."

Joe sat quietly, looking at his untouched plate. He shifted his gaze to his pale hands and then under the table to his twisted leg. He sat still for a long time.

"Aunt Cinthia—"

"Yes, Joe?"

"I been studying with Uncle Toby a long time. I know a lot of things now. I'm going to take his place as well as I can."

"No! You aren't strong!"

"Maybe I can make up with this what I lack there." And he touched his head and indicated his leg. "We've got to keep eating, Aunt Cinthia."

"The farm—"

"Never brings in any cash. I'll figure out . . ." He lifted his head and listened to a rig roll up. He gathered his crutch under his armpit and went to the door.

A big man, plump and friendly, shook Joe's hand and came in. "Howdy, Mrs. Cinthia."

"Mr. Dawson!" said Aunt Cinthia. She was a little overcome because Mr. Dawson was the biggest lawyer in the county and had once been a representative in the State legislature. "Sit down!"

Mr. Dawson bowed and sat down. "You are looking prettier than ever these days, Mrs. Cinthia," said Mr. Dawson.

Aunt Cinthia blushed and got Mr. Dawson some coffee.

"You look right well, Joe," said Mr. Dawson.

"Thank you," said Joe. "I'm going to give this crutch to Jeb for toothpicks one of these days. You'll see."

"Good spirit," said Mr. Dawson. He drank his coffee and gradually became forlorn of countenance to prepare them for his business. After a long time he looked fixedly at Aunt Cinthia.

"I came here to do some business for Toby," said Mr. Dawson. He was sure of their attention and went on. "A long

44

time ago, Toby came to me and told me that he wanted to leave his will with me."

Aunt Cinthia blew her nose on her apron and managed to stifle the sobs which welled up in her. "Uncle Toby was a good man, Mr. Dawson."

"The whole country around and about couldn't have been wrong," said Mr. Dawson. "He was a very fine man. He told me that one of these days he might not turn up alive in the morning, and so he thought I had better take care of things for him. Of course, he isn't legally dead. Won't be for years. But that was his wish that the will would be read if he was gone as long as fifteen days. It is, I believe, sixteen since last he was seen."

Aunt Cinthia swallowed hard. Joe rattled his crutch and cleared his throat.

"So he gave me this will of his. I'm not going to pester you with legal terms. I'm going to tell you what it says. He leaves to you, Mrs. Cinthia, as his wife, the whole farm and all and any of his property. He didn't have any money to leave. All his property except one thing and that he leaves to Joe."

Joe looked wonderingly at Mr. Dawson. Uncle Toby didn't have any property except the farm and a few clothes and his instruments.

"To you," said Mr. Dawson, "Toby leaves his room."

"What?" said Joe.

"He leaves his room and everything in it," said Mr. Dawson, "to you on the condition that you keep it more or less as it is, that you allow no one else in it for any length of time and that you absolutely forbid and enforce the law that it is not to be cleaned. He said a man needs a place to crawl off. And be all by himself and think things out. And so he leaves you his room. That's all there is in the will."

Aunt Cinthia began to weep and kept on weeping even after Mr. Dawson had gone. Joe sat in front of the stove until nearly midnight. Until that will had been read he had had some faint hope. But now it became a certain fact that he would never again see Uncle Toby, never again hear him chuckle, never again be given a new book with heavily underscored lines.

The next afternoon Joe limped into the house, more weary and discouraged than ever before in his life. He did not feel like hitching himself any farther than the kitchen, but he could not endure, he realized suddenly, the inquiring and sad eyes of Aunt Cinthia. Joe bethought himself of the room, and, saying nothing, dragged himself through the parlor, thrust the door shut and sank down in Uncle Toby's—now Joe's—chair.

For a little while he didn't look at anything. But as the gloom rested his eyes and the coolness caressed his brow he pulled papers out of his pocket and threw them on the desk.

Those bills were worthless. In two places Joe had brought himself to ask for money only to find the subject slid away unremarked and some ailing pigs substituted. Joe had not collected any money. But he had treated the pigs. This mass of paper represented a lifetime of unpaid work. Lunches, seed, harness buckles, night lodgings, a few fresh vegetables and odds and ends had been the only pay Uncle Toby had ever collected so far as Joe could see.

He sat there and looked at his twisted leg. Uncle Toby had kept the farmers of this county in solvency by keeping their stock in good condition and the farmers of this county had never done anything tangible for Uncle Toby. That had become very plain.

Joe wondered if he would feel such a responsibility to the community that he would keep on as Uncle Toby had. But Uncle Toby had never mentioned money to Joe and evidently had never asked anyone for money and yet Uncle Toby had been contented and cheerful. There was a puzzle here.

Was service to the community enough recompense?

Joe absently took a pipe out of his pocket and spent some time fumbling for his tobacco before he remembered that he had, that day, run out. On the chance that there was some in the room he looked about, got up and approached the cabinet.

He had never been in here more than twice and then he had not seen anything strange. But these little boxes and vials, all so artfully done, carved and molded were far from usual. They seemed to be empty, most of them, and their shapes and purposes defied speculation. They were pretty. That was all. One jar was heavy and Joe lifted the lid to find his tobacco. The aroma was pleasantly fresh, a little sweet and recalled nostalgically, Uncle Toby. Joe spilled a few crumbs filling his pipe and these mingled with what had been spilled when he had lifted off the lid. The container was heavy pottery and the lid was the cap of a clown.

Joe sat down and picked up a big match. He dodged back, startled, for the thing had lighted as soon as he brought it near his pipe. He picked it up from where he had dropped it and

47

shakily applied the flame. It was a most curious circumstance. There were many other matches, similar to it, in the alabaster hand which served as a holder and Joe picked up another one. As he brought it near his pipe it did not light. Nor would it light when he scratched it under the desk. The stove door was open to furnish a draft of cool air and Joe threw the match into it. As soon as it struck the grate it lighted.

But Joe was too weary to speculate much. He was tired. Terribly, sickeningly tired. The hot sun, the smell of the sties, the long ride in the jolting buggy had been more exertion than he had had in many months. Such activity was strictly against Uncle Toby's orders.

There was a tall bottle, glitteringly cut with faces, standing on the top of the roll-top desk. The amber in it looked as though it would pick a man out of his blues and Joe poured a liberal potion into a matching glass. The bottle had been full to the cork and for a little while, as he sipped his drink, he did not notice that the bottle was still full. When he did notice he put down the glass as though it had scorched him. He sat for a short time and then poured another potion. The bottle was still full.

He corked it tightly and turned it around and around in his hands while the little glass faces seemed to smile companionably at him. This was very excellent, but very ordinary bourbon, and this seemed to be a wholly sane bottle. Joe put it back. He felt a little tingle at the back of his neck.

Not so tired now, he began to sense this room. Once before he had noticed that a deep and quiet peace filled the place, that no harsh sounds came here, that it was cool when the day was hot and warm when the wintery blasts chilled the plains. And now he felt that abiding sense of safety and well-being once more.

Maybe it was because Uncle Toby had been so calm, so cheerful. Maybe he had left that impression in this place.

Cautiously, Joe resumed his drink and, as the languorous minutes went by, emptied it.

He was startled into chattering terror when the bottle swooped down and filled the glass again of its own accord. But plucking up courage he took the bottle in hand, found no strings or mechanisms and felt the tingle on the back of his neck grow. Still he could not be wholly afraid.

This time a tiny inscription caught his attention. Graven upon the glowing bottom of the bottle were the words:

To Uncle Toby
With blessings
From Princess Dundein

Joe read it over and over and set the bottle down to think, for he had never heard Uncle Toby mention anyone by the name of Princess Dundein. And the only princesses in Laudon County were show horses.

With no new thought after much effort, Joe got up and filled his pipe at the cabinet. Then he frowned and removed the clown's cap a second time. Yes, he was right! The tobacco jar was full again. He had used two pipes from it now and yet when the cap was pulled off the tobacco always spilled!

He looked carefully at the jar. The clown's face seemed to stretch into a wider smile. In gold, upon the side, was minutely written:

To my good friend Toby
From Ysytsfrau

Certainly no one by that name had ever come to Palmerville. And certainly Uncle Toby had never traveled to a land where such a word would be common.

Joe tucked his crutch tighter under his armpit and carefully put the jar back in its place. He could not be sure, but he was afraid the clown had winked at him.

There were other knick-knacks now that he looked. From lord, king, duchess or ladies. And all to their dearest, or respected and admired, Toby or Uncle Toby. There was a perfume container which played music as it sprayed and made rainbows in its mist. There was a little ring which spread a sphere of light. There was an apple which, no matter how often or hard it was bitten or eaten, always remained itself. There was a little golden monkey which did tricks endlessly and wittily and finished up by grinning for applause and then resumed its metallic inanimacy. There was a book which read poetry aloud in a soothing, feminine voice and a little muezzin which called out a strange-tongued phrase and turned ever in a certain direction no matter which way he was set down.

Joe grew tired. He could not be afraid of these things, they were all so cheerful and pleasant. Dazedly he went out to supper and heard not a word that Aunt Cinthia said.

There were other knick-knacks now that he looked.
From lord, king, duchess or ladies. And all to their dearest,
or respected and admired, Toby or Uncle Toby.

Several days passed before Joe discovered anything further about the room.

He had found that persistence in driving about the country and working was being rewarded at least by gains in his own health for, though nothing could ever cure his twisted leg, sunshine and air could cure his pallor and association with many other people could gradually work away his shyness. He had promised to look again at the pigs he had treated and the second calls had resulted in further calls. Because there seemed to be very little he could do to escape, he found himself gradually coming into possession of Uncle Toby's wholly unremunerative practice.

As Joe explained it to Aunt Cinthia, "They ask and—well, it would be sort of insulting to Uncle Toby if I said 'no.'"

He had read and listened to Uncle Toby and had treated livestock himself, so it was not hard to keep up with these simple ailments. The farmers had always had considerable respect for his learning, judging from the correct use he made of speech. And the fact that he was treating living things, seemed to react upon him as though he also treated himself. He could never part with his crutch, but the time came when he did not wince when he walked.

Aunt Cinthia was very quiet these days, her eyes lighting only when a step sounded upon the back porch—to darken when she discovered it was not Uncle Toby. She grew thin and preoccupied and the veins stuck out on her huge red hands and little spots of unnatural color stood high on her cheekbones in sharp contrast to the gray hollows below. Joe began to worry about her for it was very plain to him at least that Aunt Cinthia, inch by inch, was pulling a shroud over herself. But she would not talk very much and his presence did not seem to comfort her. More and more time he spent in Toby's room while Aunt Cinthia sat listlessly in the kitchen.

It was comforting to Joe to have a place into which he could crawl and where he could quietly think about things. And through the long days of driving and talking he always had a small part of his mind fixed upon the comfort and relief of the dim silence of the room.

With his crutch propped against the desk, Joe would lean back in the unstable chair and gaze at the knick-knacks in the cabinet. He liked to puzzle upon their sources, upon the identities of the kings and lords and princesses and ladies who had so graciously inscribed them, and he began to build faces and manners to fit the names and gifts. It never actually occurred to Joe that he might encounter the sources.

Perhaps he would have gone on pondering the matter for years if, one day, he had not forgotten to tell Aunt Cinthia in passing that Mrs. Barthlomew had said she would send over a cake. Joe had come straight to the room, and closed the door and had seated himself at the desk. And then he remembered.

With a sigh he picked up his crutch again, hauled himself to his feet and went back to the door. He opened it and walked out.

For ten steps at least he was blinded by preoccupation. He did not notice that he was not walking through the parlor until he moved aside to pass the center table. The center table was not there!

The greenish light about him startled him. He looked up and gazed a limitless distance through green water. He looked down and saw that he stood upon current-smoothed coral. He looked around and saw that he was in an undersea garden, where tall green plumes swept gracefully from side to side in slow motion and where gay little fish lurked nervously behind the colorful pinnacles of rock.

In a sudden panic Joe stumped in a half circle and tried to regain the door. It was there. The room was beyond it, clearly visible.

Joe was afraid to breathe. The solidity of the water did not seem to interfere with his return. He gained the door and slammed it shut, standing there with his back against it for a long time, trying to regain his composure.

The curiousness of the situation was a long time in coming to him and then he began to be interested in the defiance of the law of physics. The water had not flowed into this place at all. That heartened him. That made things seem better, somehow. That gave the water a friendly and thoughtful aspect.

Cautiously, Joe opened the door a crack. He peeked out. But no undersea garden was there now. There was the organ, there were the album and the Bible, there were the false flowers under their glass domes and the clock which wouldn't run. It was the parlor again.

Joe closed the door, waited a moment and again opened it. The parlor was still there.

That night at supper it was on his lips to tell Aunt Cinthia about this singular circumstance, but on considering, he decided that it would only worry her, and so kept his own counsel. Jeb picked his teeth with thoroughness. Aunt Cinthia cleared away the dishes. Nobody said anything.

Jeb finished picking his teeth and went out to admire the night. Joe rubbed his palm thoughtfully against the top of his crutch and listened to the dishes rattling in the sink.

Three nights passed before Joe received any other surprises in Uncle Toby's room. He had nearly given up hope, for once his initial fear had vanished he had found in himself a considerable thirst for further investigation into that undersea garden. Each evening he had closed the door to quickly open it again. Each evening he had been greeted by the musty staleness of the parlor.

He began to get exasperated.

And then, when his patience was translucent with thinness, he determined that he would not further investigate. On this evening he came into the room, closed the door, eased himself into the chair and placed his crutch against the desk. He took a long breath and let his nerves relax. He looked at the door with a grimace and refused to be lured for he knew that if he again opened it he would find only the parlor, the organ, the album, the Bible and the glass domes over the artificial flowers. He settled himself to think about the strange ailment which had taken possession of Mr. Carmody's prize stallion and the unanswerable listlessness which had overcome George Stockwell's cow.

The bottle swept down off the desk top and poured out a glass. Joe ignored it. The monkey went through an exhausting series of convulsions and Joe paid no heed. The book persisted in reading poetry and he dropped it into a drawer from which came out muffled and plaintive tones as soon as it was closed.

He would not be lured and laughed at.

But within a few minutes he was at the door, hand on the knob, pulling it open.

The light, hot and golden, blinded him. He blinked at the smoldering wastes which stretched rollingly away to a cluster of scrawny palms and at the gas-flame sky from which scorched down a high-noon equatorial sun.

Joe hitched his crutch close into his armpit and went a few steps in the yielding sand. The dunes before him made small mountains and deep valleys and ten thousand glass snakes writhed in a quiet dance.

The door was behind him. It, with its casement, stood all by itself.

Joe went up the side of a dune with great difficulty and stood looking into the depression beyond, not much surprised to see a small party of horsemen there at the head of a laden camel train.

The leader raised his gun in salute and Joe raised his crutch. The horses spurted into a gallop and labored up the slope, sinking to the knee in loose sand at each lunge.

"Hello," said the leader. He was swarthy and his light blue eyes contrasted weirdly with his complexion. He rested his rifle across the pommel of his silver-worked saddle and threw back the hood of his djellaba.

"Hello," said Joe.

"Where is Uncle Toby?" said the leader.

"I was going to ask you," said Joe.

"You mean he is gone somewhere?"

"He has been gone for a long time," said Joe.

The leader turned to the curtained box which rode the back of a big, white camel. "He says Uncle Toby is gone."

A pair of eyes, lighter and bluer than the leader's, looked carefully through a slit in the finely brocaded cloth. "Where did he go?" said a soft, woman's voice.

"He says he doesn't know," stated the leader.

There was a sigh. And then the eyes played with interest on Joe. It was a new experience for Joe to find himself looked at without any trace of pity.

The woman said, "Leave the things, anyway. You, what is his name, Abd?"

"Joe," said Joe.

"You will be back again, Joe?" said the woman.

"Yes," said Joe.

"Leave him the things, Abd. Tell him if he sees Uncle Toby to tell him we will miss him."

"She says that we miss Uncle Toby and she is right," the leader told Joe.

Three riders swung down and took a small silver box and a red satin bag from the camel packs. They carried these to the door and put them down. They bowed very low to Joe and mounted again.

The leader saluted. The woman waved. The cavalcade moved briskly away.

Joe stood there for a little while with the hot desert wind drying out his skin. Then he went back and picked up the silver box and the red satin bag. He went through the door and closed it behind him.

For a little while he stood looking at the room and thinking about Uncle Toby and then from somewhere came the dinner gong which Aunt Cinthia was ringing for Jeb to come up from the evening chores.

Joe put the silver box on the top of the cabinet. He put his hand into the silken bag and pulled out a heavy weight of coins. He looked at them, jingling them on his palm, not much surprised to find it was perfectly good money.

He put the coins into his pocket and opened the door. The parlor was dim and stale and the crayon portrait of Uncle Toby on the wall looked stiffly at him. Joe could not be sure about the smile he felt had crossed the picture.

When he sat down to the table, Jeb was already eating, with some slight suction. Aunt Cinthia piled mashed potatoes on Joe's plate and gave him a slab of meat.

Aunt Cinthia, as time flowed onward, drew more and more from her own company until she seemed to wear a cloak of silence through which nothing could penetrate. Methodically and tiredly she went on with her endless tasks, bending her tallness over tubs and sink and stove.

She gradually developed a strange fascination for sunsets, standing on the porch each evening to watch the great globe halve, quarter and vanish behind the prairie rim. There seemed to be considerable satisfaction for her in thus watching the days vanish one by one, to see the changes of winter into spring, spring into summer, summer into fall and fall again into winter. And as time went by, Joe began to notice that the only hope in her eyes shone there in the brief moment of the dying light.

It was not much of a surprise to Joe, then, when he came one dusky winter evening up the road to the house and found Aunt Cinthia sitting relaxed and apparently quite comfortably upon the back porch, oblivious to the severe chill in the wind. He spoke to her and shook her shoulder.

When her head fell back, Joe found himself looking into her peaceful eyes. Aunt Cinthia was dead.

Palmerville and Laudon County had very little to say about it. People went to the funeral and said the properly doleful things to Joe and then for a few Sundays after remarked the clean whiteness of the new cross in the churchyard. Then they forgot about her.

Joe kept on doctoring pigs, driving around the country, speaking pleasantly to everyone and leaning easily upon his crutch. Joe never talked about himself or what he did, but that was all right for other people were too willing to talk about themselves and didn't notice. Nobody paid Joe. Everyone depended upon him and respected what he said. Nobody had anything to do with a new veterinary from State who tried to hang up a shingle in Palmerville. Joe was part of the community, like the church steeple and the old elm at the end of the bridge.

But things change even in places like Palmerville. Things change and things happen.

Jeb, an old man now, came into town one morning with the news that Joe had vanished.

People were excited about it for a little while and went looking under bushes and culverts and not much work was done for three days.

And then something else happened. Joe's house, without cause, caught on fire and burned right to the foundation to leave two chimneys sticking up out of charcoal like a pair of self-appointed sentries.

Nobody rebuilt the house. Nobody ever found Joe.

Five or six years later when a farmer, who had gotten rich, decided he had better atone for some things he maybe shouldn't have done, work was started on a new church to replace the old frame building which had weathered so much petty sin. The work necessitated the moving of a few graves, and among those was that where Aunt Cinthia had been buried.

The workmen very nearly had the coffin buried again when one fellow, more observant than the rest, discovered that the coffin was empty.

People talked about it for a little while and then, because babies were getting born and crops had to be sown and reaped and chores had to be done, forgot about that, also.

He Didn't Like Cats

He Didn't Like Cats

A wise man could have told Jacob Findley that vindictiveness is usually synonymous with downfall, even vindictiveness in minute things. But Jacob Findley lived in Washington, DC.

Ordinarily, Jacob took from life all its faults without complaint, for as a civil servant of the United States he was inured to many things and, through practice, quite complaisant in general. But, perhaps, bottling official insults within himself was not wholly possible since common logic tells one that a vessel can be filled just so full, after which it leaks or overflows. Jacob was not the type of man to overflow. Cup by cup he was filled; somewhere along the route from desk to desk in his department he had to have a means of release.

People in official positions quite often pass down in kind what is received from above and Jacob, as a file clerk, was down so low that it was most difficult to find a means of spilling.

So he didn't like cats.

A more defeated and resigned man would have been difficult to find, for he was a veritable sponge for abuse. His hair was graying, his eyes downcast, his walk a slouch and even his clothes had a tired air.

But he didn't like cats.

His was not a vindictive nature. In most things he was patiently kind, Joblike enduring. He often gave candy to little children, quite strangers to him. While it might be said that his generosity was more like the offering of tribute in turn for immunity, it was still generosity.

However—or perhaps, therefore—he did not like cats.

Tonight he was in an average mood. The day had been tedious, monotonous, wearying. And tonight he was on his way to attend a church supper which, because he would be, as usual, forgotten in the midst of many, would be tedious, monotonous, wearying.

Clad in a shiny tuxedo, topped by a rusty derby, swinging his cane in halfhearted imitation of his office chief at the State Department, he walked patiently up Sixteenth Street toward the Lutheran church, pausing obediently at all the lights, absence of cars notwithstanding on the lettered streets. A steady parade of cabs and limousines coursed busily upon his left, discordantly giving forth blasts of radio music, a blast bracketed in silence either side, and yelps or laughter or conversation.

He had just crossed N Street when he met his fa—when he met the cat.

It was not a polite meeting nor a sociable contact, for the cat arrogantly ignored Jacob Findley and issued from an apartment-house shrub to lay its course across the bows of the man.

As cats went, he was at best a second-rate feline in looks, but in the cat world he must have been singularly respected if his tattered and scarred condition was any indication of victories hardly won. He was a huge cat, a dirty cat and a very proud cat. He was missing half his right ear, several of his port whiskers, a third of his right forefoot and about a sixteenth of his tail, to say nothing of patches where fur had been. His air was gladiatorial, for he strutted rather than walked, and there was a vain heft to his brows which bespoke his disdain for cats less proficient in the art of plying claw and tooth and for all humans without any exception. Here was a cat that was tough and proud of it, but which had commingled with that toughness a wary glance for possible enemies and a lewd leer in event he passed any ladies.

Jacob was so overlaid with strata of servility that only a sharp start could have brought him leaping out of himself the way he leaped. The cat startled him, for he supposed in the brief glimpse he had that he was about to trip over some treacherous object.

Then he saw that it was a cat.

He realized that he had been startled by a cat.

And, as the reader might have gathered, he did not like cats.

"Scat!" cried Jacob Findley.

The feline pursued his swashbuckling way, his strut a bit more pronounced. This effrontery yanked Jacob Findley even further out of himself, far enough for him to act wholly on impulse.

He aimed a kick at the cat. It was not a ferocious kick. It was not even intended to land. But Findley had been led this far to his doom and any momentum yet wanting, fate seemed to supply.

The cat received a sharp black toe in his side. He swooped

upward with it, draped inextricably over it. He received the inertia thus imparted to him and described a parabola streetward. The cat sought to twist in the air and fall short, but doom was now on the march. The noisy, swift traffic coursed along Sixteenth Street. The cat lit in the road and, having lit, tried to scramble back to the curb.

A tire rocketed catward. The whole car vibrated to the jolt. And then it jolted again.

Clawing and crying, the cat struggled to reach the gutter, hitching himself inch by inch. He was out of the way of further wheels now, but he had done himself an unkindness. His back was broken so that while his hind legs lay twisted to the right, his forefeet convulsed toward the left.

The cat's cry stretched dismally.

Jacob Findley was confused. He was shamed. The agony of the animal reached him and made him shudder and sweat. Having just committed the most violent and wanton act of his life, he felt ill.

He felt his drums would burst under the onslaught of that cry, and it seemed to him that there were words in it, human words and curses.

Gradually the wail changed and faded and then it was as if the cat had truly found, in his death throes, a human voice. But there were no words. Only agony.

Jacob Findley heard the rattling last of it. He trembled.

And then, savage that he should be made to feel so, he stalked angrily upon his way, angrily stating to himself that, for all that, he *still* didn't *like* cats.

"Good riddance," said Jacob Findley. That heartened him.

A cat was a cat and that one had been a filthy and useless cat. He got braver. He turned and looked back toward the shadow in the gutter and raised his voice.

"Good riddance!" jeered Jacob Findley.

He went on and every time a shudder sought to rise along his spine, he was there with another statement as to the uselessness of cats in general and of that cat in particular. Still—what had that cat said when—

"Served him right," growled Findley.

Funny, though, how those yowls had sounded—

"Mangiest cat I ever saw. Better off dead, damn him!"

Two wheels had hit it and yet what a long time it had taken to die! It had even been able to move and—

"Hah, hah," said Jacob Findley with false merriment. "I guess I used up all his nine lives in a batch. Damn him!"

Had he been in error when he had supposed the cat to stare at him, glare at him even in its death—

"Try to run over me, would he? Well, I guess I finished him. Yes, sir! I guess I finished him, all right, all right. Deadest cat I ever saw. Damn him!"

Odd how there had been words in that agonized scream—

"Made enough noise for fifteen cats. Hah, hah. Maybe he had to die nine times and so made nine times as much noise. Cats like that bother me? Not on your life. Kick dozens of them under trucks. Dozens of them. Make recordings of their voices and listen to them of an evening. Yah! Damned, mangy, good-for-nothing *cat*!"

What had that cat said when it was dying?

Why, Jacob Findley! Whatever are you muttering about?"

Jacob nearly leaped from his cracked shoes, shying away from the voice. With foolish relief he saw that it was Bessy Green who spoke, and that he had come into the church hall without realizing it. In fact, he had even checked his hat and cane and stood now at the entrance to the lower room which was being used for the supper dance. However had he gotten this far without knowing it?

His perturbation was nearly extinguished by the realization that Bessy Green was smiling at him and chattering on in a merry fashion. This was an oddity, indeed, for while she had never snubbed him, she had never paid any attention to him, either.

She was a secretary to an official in the Interior Department, employed more because of efficiency than beauty. She was climbing up toward retirement age, and her forthcoming pension had been a target for much amorous attention. She had a fault of wearing too much makeup, poorly applied, and had a head of somewhat scarce hair which she had dyed black.

Jacob's astonishment at her attention was born from the knowledge that she had been receiving for a long time the court of one Krantz, a guard at the Department of Commerce.

"And I think it is wicked! Terribly, terribly wicked! There are so few men in Washington as it is and then this silly draft sweeps away those who are here. But Joe said that his duty was with his country and so he left. A dear, dear boy, Jacob, but I don't think I shall ever forgive him."

"The country must be served," said Jacob, having overheard that this day from the protocol.

"Ah, yes, the country must be served. And here we poor lonely women, bereft, must also stand back with bowed heads and submit. Ah, yes. If it weren't for my cats I should be terribly, terribly, terribly lonely."

"Cats?" gulped Jacob.

"Ah, yes, the poor dear things. Isn't it strange how you just can't keep from loving them? You do love cats, don't you, Jacob?"

Jacob blinked rapidly. He kept his wits, however, for attention from Bessy Green was to be valued and her pension was not uninvolved as a factor in her charm.

"Cats?" said Jacob. "Oh, yes, yes, yes. Cats. Certainly I am fond of cats. Shall we dance, Miss Green?"

They danced and Jacob concentrated hard upon the effort, for he was experiencing a great desire not to step upon her or lose the rhythm. Along the sidelines ladies and the sparse scattering of men looked on and there was much behind-hand talking.

One woman in particular remarked the intimate way Miss Green was whispering into Jacob's ear and this one woman, Doris Hanson, sat more alertly and her eyes took on a faintly greenish hue. Rival for Krantz, Doris Hanson was not to allow a second male to get securely into the hands of *that woman.*

Quite by accident Doris Hanson was near when the music stopped and Jacob and Bessy walked from the floor. Doris Hanson was a heavily built, purposeful woman whose ideas were intensely practical. She fancied herself as a psychologist, for she had attended a night university for years and years and years.

"Why, Jacob!" said Doris. "I am so happy to see you!"

Jacob was confused. He had never been noticed by Doris Hanson before. In fact, because she was noted as a brainy woman, he had been in fear of her.

"You look," said Doris Hanson, "exceedingly well tonight. But then, of course, you always look splendid. Oh, how do you do, Miss Green?"

"I do very well," said Miss Green.

The two women smiled at each other. Jacob felt chilly.

"Ah, the music! The 'Tiger Rag'!" said Doris. "My favorite song."

Jacob did not know quite how it had happened, but he found himself being thrust about the floor by this amazon and was aware of acute displeasure from the direction of Bessy Green.

So overwhelmed had he been by such attention that he had nearly forgotten the cat.

He was reminded.

In the piece being played were certain trumpet slurs which were, at first, only jarring to Jacob. And then, little by little, those slurs and wails and cries began to eat into his ears and touch there sympathetic vibrations which, sent again into motion, caused him to behold and hear the dying cat. He grew nervous and if he sagged a little bit, Doris Hanson did not notice.

"Hold that tiger! *EEEeeeyow!* Hold that tiger! *EEEEEEEEEEEeeeeeyow—*"

Jacob felt himself getting ill. Why did they have to keep doing it, bar after bar! Chorus after chorus!

"Hold that tiger! *EEEEEEEEEEEEEEEEEEE eeeeeeYOW!* Hold—"

Had he been a less repressed individual, he might have plugged his ears or screamed or damned the orchestra, for now it began to seem to him as if the cat himself was up there in the box, glaring gloatingly about the floor after Jacob and taking high glee in mocking him.

"Hold that tiger! *Eeeeeeeyow!* Hold that tiger! *EEEEEEEEEEEEEYOWWWWWWWWW!*"

He could see the cat! On the bandstand!

And on that instant the music stopped and Jacob, adrip with perspiration, goggled confusedly at the musicians. No cat. Just some fellows with trumpets and drums.

Feeling ill and weak, he was glad of Doris Hanson's support, given quite unconsciously. He was dragged from the floor and again found himself surrounded by the two women. He hardly noticed either of them as he sank into a chair and they, interested in the battle more than the spoils, did not notice his state.

Jacob became angry with himself and commenced to form chains of invective in which to bind the cat.

"And it was an intensely interesting trip," said Doris Hanson. "I don't know when I have ever been so intrigued! It is not usual to be permitted to get into St. Elizabeth's, you know, but I knew a brother of the director—"

"I went visiting there once," said Bessy Green. "Of a Sunday. The public is always admitted on a Sunday—"

"Of course!" said Doris. "But not admitted to the halls, to the corridors, to the very cells of the unfortunate people. As a student of psychiatry I, of course, had a greater insight into the difficulties of attempting to bring sanity back to the poor unfortunates."

"I went there one Sunday," interposed Bessy Green. "I saw a man who was pushing a wheelbarrow, but he had it upside down. And if anybody asked him why he had it upside down, he looked sly and said if he turned it right side up, why, somebody might put something in it. Isn't that funny, Jacob?"

Jacob dutifully, if weakly, laughed.

"He," said Doris Hanson in a superior way, "had a persecution complex. It was fortunate you did not press him for an explanation, for they very often require very little to become violent, just as they require little to become insane."

"B-Beg pardon?" said Jacob.

"Oh, you have no idea," said Doris, gripping and nearly strangling this spark of interest from the quarry. "In just such a way are some people touched off. Insanity may lie latent and unsuspected in a disposition for years and then, suddenly, *poof!* a full case of dementia praecox!"

"Just . . . *poof*?" said Jacob.

Doris quickly laughed, an eye on Bessy. "You are so droll, Jacob. Just . . . *poof!*"

"I . . . really wanted to know," said Jacob.

"It's true," replied Doris with a sniff in Bessy's direction to make her sensible of a victory, even if a minor one. "It is amazing how so many people go insane. One day a man is a normal, friendly husband and the next he suddenly becomes a raging schizoid and slays his wife and himself as well. The result of what cause? Why, perhaps he chanced to find some schoolgirl treasure of another beau who had been his greatest rival and is stunned to discover that she secretly retains this. But usually the matter is not so simple, you know. Next to nothing may happen, jarring awake some sleeping monstrosity in a man's complex mental machinery and turning him from a sane person to a mentally sick individual. It is wholly impossible to say when a man is sane, for"—she tittered—"scarce one of us is normal."

"You mean—it might happen to any of us?"

"Of course," said Doris, charmed by all this interest. "One moment we are seated here, behaving normally, and the next some tiny thing, a certain voice, a certain combination of thoughts, may throw out the balance wheel of our intellects and we become potential inmates for asylums the rest of our lives. No, not one of us knows when the world will cease to be a normal, ordinary place. You know, no one ever knows when he goes insane. He supposes it is the world altering, not himself. Rooms become peopled with strange shapes and beings, sounds distort themselves into awful cries and, *poof!* we are judged insane."

"*Poof . . .*" said Jacob, feeling weak and ill.

Bessy smiled acidly sweet upon Doris. "Of course that is the tenet of 'modern science,' but there are yet other explanations, you know." She gave Jacob a comforting look.

"Other? I am not aware of mumbo jumbo—"

"Not mumbo jumbo," Bessy interrupted her. "I happen to be a very advanced student of spiritualism and it is quite likely that insane people see and hear beings and actualities which

73

are more than the twisted ideas of deranged intellects. If one cares to extend his study beyond mere daily conceptions, he can swiftly realize the immense probability and possibility of such. Belief in evil spirits is too persistent in the history of man to be easily discounted, and it is my belief that our 'insane asylums' house many who are, to be blunt, too psychic."

"Too . . . psychic?" said Jacob.

"Why, yes. They see and perceive things which are beyond the sight and perception of the ordinary, crass intellect and so are judged, or rather misjudged, by their fellow humans. Ghosts, angry spirits, avenging demons, it is wholly probable that these things exist in truth."

"Exist?" echoed Jacob.

"Wholly possible," said Bessy with a jerk of her sparse, dyed head.

Under this onslaught, calculated to attack and discredit her by doing that to her tenets, Doris remained wholly aloof as though such things were completely ridiculous and beneath any natural consideration.

"Then . . . then things can haunt people?" managed Jacob.

"Naturally," said Bessy, "and I have no doubt at all that many is the murderer who has been driven to the grave by the avenging spirit of his victim!"

"H-How?"

"You have heard of men turning themselves in to the police and confessing crimes which were not otherwise to be solved?" said Bessy. "You have heard of murderers eventually seeing the faces of their victims in everything about them? Very well. Is it not just as possible that the murdered being appeared to him? Or at least caused events and impressions to surround the criminal until the criminal considered himself better off dead?"

"Rubbish," said Doris.

"I beg pardon?" said Bessy.

"I said rubbish! The words of our most learned doctors put everything you say back into the Dark Ages!"

"And the wisest of them all," said Bessy grimly, "has no knowledge or experience of philosophy!"

"That is not philosophy!" said Doris. "That is stupid African voodoo rubbish!"

"If it is," said Bessy, "then our finest physicists are heading straight for African voodoo rubbish every time they admit that beyond a certain point, no knowledge can be gained at all without the admission of God."

"What has God to do with this?" said Doris.

"God has everything to do with it, since he is the regulating factor of the universe, and if he chooses to drive men mad with the appearance of evil beings and avenging spirits, then dare you deny his ability to do so?"

Doris opened her mouth to speak and then saw the cunningness of this trap. Almost she had allowed herself to give forth blasphemy. Her wit was not agile enough to encompass a countermeasure and she did not dare sniff lest that, too, be accounted blasphemy.

They had argued longer than Doris had supposed, for it was with surprise that she heard the music stop and saw that the supper had been laid out. Thankful for this she rose.

"I shall bring you something, Jacob," said Doris and departed.

Jacob would have protested that food would stick in his throat and lie heavily in his stomach, but he had not the energy to protest. Accordingly he was soon holding a plate which was heaping with lobster salad. He felt it would be an insult to Doris not to eat it. Slowly, he ate it. Thankfully he got rid of the last mouthful. Shudderingly he put the plate away.

Bessy leaped up and seized the plate. "Oh, I must get you some more!" And she hurried away to come back in a moment with an even larger portion and a glare for Doris.

Jacob knew he could not refuse. Manfully he marshaled his willpower and concentration. He began to eat.

"Speculation in the realm of the Unknowable is a fruitless folly," stated Doris, fondly rolling the words around in her mouth. "Men can only grasp what they can sense. Hence, having sensed a thing, a man cannot lose his belief in it until he has proof which can also be sensed!"

"Ah," glittered Bessy. "What a simple way to deny the existence of everything which man, in his benighted mortal mind, cannot sense! What a charming way to dispose of God!"

"Oh, no!" said Doris.

"Oh, yes," said Bessy, having found the Achilles' heel and now not letting go. "You deny the mind any other power than its material senses. In such a way you dare not dispose of the soul! Man's immortal spirit is within him and he is in contact with it and it is in contact with the Immensity of God. With the Immensity of God," she repeated, liking the term. "Belief in itself has performed many miracles and I do not think one dares take it upon herself to deny the Bible."

"Certainly not!" said Doris, angrily wondering how she could get out of this trap.

"The mind, properly attuned, can become One with All, for man, in the image of God, is certainly a servant of God if he so wishes."

"Naturally, but—"

"And as God can create, so can man create," stated Bessy. "There are miracles and miracles to prove that. Even modern miracles. Faith is belief, and if a man can believe anything enough, then certainly that thing becomes an actuality."

"But—" limped Doris.

"The mind of man, becoming attuned to the All, is, of course, endowed with some of the Power of God. For example, if a man desires a thing enough, then that thing is his. In a sense he has created that thing and his desire for it has altered or shaped it to his liking. A man can create out of his own belief just as God can create, for man is one with the Universe and the Universe is God. Any belief, intense enough, creates actuality." She smiled sweetly upon Jacob, who had now manfully managed the second plate. "Would you have some dessert?"

Jacob was too dazed to protest, physically and mentally slugged into resistlessness. He was trying to rally, but rally he could not, since it weighed upon him that he would somehow have to eat the dessert as well.

Bessy came back and placed it before him. Exerting all the last dregs of determination he sat up, raised the spoon to attack the ice cream and then shuddered.

77

A cookie lay there. A cookie which was cut in the shape of a *cat*. And even as he looked, the cookie seemed to grin at him.

"Ooooooooooooooh," said Jacob and quietly collapsed.

They escorted him home in a cab, both of them apparently concerned about his condition, but nevertheless finding much time to glare at each other over his back. Under other circumstances Jacob might have been flattered into near expansiveness, but now he was brought to such depths of misery, both physical and mental, that he scarcely heeded their solicitousness.

Of course neither of them had said a thing about that cat, and he certainly could not tell them. But now Bessy, to soothe him, began to rub in the salt.

"You will simply have to come and see my cats sometime," she was saying as the cab rolled to a halt before Jacob's door. "They are so sweet and so cute. Cats are nearly human, don't you think, Jacob?"

"Th-This is where I live," said Jacob.

Supporting himself by gripping the doorknob, he managed to wave good night to them and call out a feeble thanks. At the bottom of the steps they both turned and nodded and then went their separate ways.

"Meow," said a night prowler in the gloom.

Jacob let himself into the house and dashed up the steps so fast that he was in his room, with door closed and bolted, before the animal had finished the final syllable.

"You are being foolish," said Jacob. "You are being very

silly. It is not true what Bessy said about evil beings. It is not true that animals have souls. It is not true that that cat could arrange a series of events after it was dead and so drive me to something desperate. What do I care about a mangy, filthy, decrepit, stupid, useless *cat*?"

Bessy was being silly. The world was a wholly rational place. Doris had the proper idea. *She* couldn't be shaken by superstitious nonsense. No, sir. Doris had good, sound, practical ideas. Scientific! That was it. Scientific. People didn't go crazy because they saw ghosts and evil beings. People went crazy because they were obsessed with an idea or something. The mind didn't create anything, either. It was just a mind, a delicate instrument which could be thrown out of adjustment by some shock—

From the backyard came a cry, *"Errrower, fsszt!"*

Jacob leaped and wrestled the window down. Shaking, he supported himself by the foot of the bed and felt the cold rivulets of sweat course down under his arms.

What had that *cat* said when it was dying?

No! He wouldn't think of it. He would whisk it from his mind forever. He would be strong and put it aside! He crawled into bed in the darkness and pulled the covers up to his chin.

The next thing he knew, he was aware of a weight upon his chest which was warm and uncomfortable. He struggled up through the layers and layers of enfolding slumber to shove restively at the thing.

His hands contacted fur!

His eyes snapped open.

There was a cat sitting upon his chest, looking at him and purring gently. He was a huge cat, a dirty cat and a very proud cat. He was missing half his right ear, several of his port whiskers, a third of his right forefoot and about a sixteenth of his tail, to say nothing of the patches where fur had been.

"SCAT!" cried Jacob.

The cat did not move, but only purred the louder. Jacob tried to leap out of bed, but he was frozen where he lay with the terror of it. There could be no mistaking this cat! It was the same cat and it was a dead cat. Its spine had been broken so that its forefeet lay in an opposite direction from his hind feet and it was dead. But it was here and it didn't look at all dead!

"Rrrrrrrrrr-rrrrrrrrrr," purred the cat.

Almost thankfully Jacob realized that this was a nightmare. It had all the peculiarities of a nightmare. The weight on his chest, the chilled feeling all over. This was a nightmare. The cat would dissolve and go away.

It wore a gentle smile which bared a pearly tooth. It seemed comfortable and well disposed.

Jacob wildly decided to lie still and let it fade away into the nothingness of his own imagination.

The cat stayed there. Jacob lay there.

And then the cat began to grow.

It grew and it grew and it grew. Its head became the size of a sugar bowl and then the size of a cantaloupe and then the size of a pumpkin. And still it grew. And still it smiled. And the purr of it was now so loud that it had begun to shake not only Jacob but the bed as well.

*Jacob tried to leap out of bed, but he was frozen
where he lay with the terror of it.
There could be no mistaking this cat!*

Now Jacob knew that it was a nightmare, but that did not mitigate his fear. It was certain to be a nightmare. He merely believed that the cat was there and that the cat was growing and so the cat was there and the cat was growing. He would suppose that the cat was not there and the cat would then go away. It was very simple.

The cat grew and grew some more. Its head became larger than a tiger's, larger than a horse's, larger than an elephant's. Its eyes were now like dinner plates and its whiskers as big as wire cables and its fur was standing all separately, each hair as large as a porcupine quill.

Jacob was looking up at its chin. A paw was on either side of him. The exposed tooth was like a marble column. The claws in its paws were sheathed sabers. Its breath was foul as a sardine can.

"RRRRRRRRRRR-RRRRRRRRR," purred the cat.

Jacob's heart was racing. He sought cautiously to draw himself upward and beyond the paws and then made a startling discovery. His hands hooked into the bed sheet very neatly. But they were hands no more. They were tiny, black paws. Gagging at the sight of them he looked at his side. It was smooth and sleek and gray. And into his vision grew his long, graceful tail!

He was a mouse between the paws of a cat!

Jacob wriggled upward to the head of the bed and dropped hurriedly down to the floor. The heavy fall stunned him, but he scuttled along the baseboard and dived into a pile of papers.

There was no sound in the room. And then came the soft footfalls of the cat, the loud snuffling of its breath. The paper rattled.

With a squeak of horror Jacob sped away, again following the baseboard in an insensate effort to locate a hole and dive to safety. But there were no holes in the baseboard. He lunged with a skidding scramble behind the leg of the bureau and, looking out, saw the feet of the stalking cat approach.

Madly Jacob gripped the scarf of the bureau, his leap successful. He scurried behind a stack of books there and crouched with fluttering heart and burning lungs. The bureau rocked. He was staring straight up at those huge eyes.

With one bat of his paw the cat sent him hurtling out into the center of the room and then leaped after him to plant, abruptly, a paw on either side of him.

Jacob trembled. He looked up at the acre of fur chest. He looked higher to the great yellow orbs which were now dilating and contracting with pleasure. The cat's tail made loud sounds as it swished and lashed back and forth.

"RRRRRRRRRR-RRRRRRRRRRR," said the cat.

Jacob played dead. He lay and shivered and played dead.

After a little, the cat arose and became interested in washing its face. Jacob hearkened to the rasp of tongue on fur and finally opened his eyes. A great cavern appeared in the cat's face as it yawned. The fences of teeth gleamed. The cat sighed and wandered away to inspect something interesting.

Now was his chance! He could make a dash for the crack under the door and get out!

He gathered himself. He leaped away. He sped like the wind toward the crack of the door. It got bigger and bigger. He was almost there! He had—

BOW!

He sped like the wind toward the crack of the door.
It got bigger and bigger. He was almost there! He had—
BOW!

With a moan Jacob rolled to his feet in the center of the room. His side was bleeding. He was bruised. His beautiful gray fur was plastered flat with blood.

The cat lay down with a paw on either side of him. It batted him to the right paw and then batted him back to the left. The saber claws drew and sheathed in sensuous delight. Back to the left paw. Then to the right paw. Dazed and aching, Jacob fainted.

After a while, he came around. He looked for the cat and could find no trace of it. Jacob was lying there, battered and bloody in the center of the room and the cat was gone! He opened the other eye. He studied the chairs. He viewed even the window ledge. Why, the cat had vanished!

Jacob gathered his long black tail about himself and crouched there, studying the exits. That crack under the door still looked good. But he was so broken up inside that he couldn't make much speed. He leaped up and raced for it.

Freedom! Liberty! He was almost there. It grew bigger and bigger. His nose could feel the rush of cold air.

BOW!

The cat had leaped down from the bed to knock him tumbling. And now the cat gathered him up in its sharp teeth and carried him back to the center of the room.

Right paw to left paw. Let him run a few inches. Snatch him back. If he lay still for a moment, he was stirred into agonized life by the teeth, and if he ran, he was knocked back by the paws.

Gasping, a mass of pain, slit and slashed and broken,

dripping with the thick glue of the cat's saliva, Jacob knew he was nearly done.

He looked across the cobbly expanse of the carpet. He looked about the immensity of his room. Heartbroken, too weary now to move, he knew his end was near.

The cat growled, angry that so little life was left in him. A mighty set of claws scraped him and took the skin from his left side. Teeth worried him. And then, once again, the cat apparently decided that he was dead. The cat got up and strolled away. It became interested in boxing the tassel which hung from the bridge lamp. It knocked a matchbox across the room and scurried after it.

Jacob hitched himself toward the crack under the door. If only he could get there. If only his broken legs would support him long enough. If only the cat would completely forget him for the seconds necessary for him to bridge this distance.

He halved the width. He quartered it. In agony, which sent waves of nausea over him, he made his broken legs support him, though now the right one showed its shattered bone. Feet to go. And then less distance and less. The cold air there began to revive him. He was going to make it, for the cat was too far away. He was going to make it. HE WAS GOING TO MAKE IT!

BOW!

The cat knocked him back into the center of the room.

Heart and body broken, Jacob lay still. The claws raked him. The teeth punctured him. He lay still.

With a bored sigh the cat opened its mouth and took in his head. There was a crunch. There was another crunch.

Jacob Findley woke up quite sound, quite whole, and—for a moment—vastly thankful that it was, to be sure, no more than a dream. Then he realized, almost simultaneously, two things: the cat had died only once, and rather quickly, and he had a perfectly correct conviction that *he*, on the other hand, would die all night, every night. . . .

Story Preview

Story Preview

NOW that you've just ventured through some of the captivating tales in the Stories from the Golden Age collection by L. Ron Hubbard, turn the page and enjoy a preview of *The Crossroads*. Join farmer Eben Smith as he heads off to the big city to trade his wagonload of produce. But he barters a lot more than goods after he stumbles across a strange crossroads in time, bargains with different cultures in alternate realities, and accidentally wreaks havoc and chaos in each.

The Crossroads

A S soon as he got to the top of the boulder-strewn hill, it became dark and he could not find any trees. As soon as he walked around the cliff on the white road and found the graves there he abandoned that section. He was just about to explore the metal road when something was seen to be moving along it. Eben went back to his wagon and waited.

It was the strangest kind of a vehicle he had ever seen for it had no wheels. It was just a big, gleaming box which scudded along the surface without a sound. There was something frightening about it.

When it came abreast of the wagon it stopped and a section of it clanked outward. A thing which was possibly a man, leaned out, staring at Eben. Its head was nearly as big as its body and it had two antennae waving above its brow as well as its huge, pupilless eyes.

"Musta escaped from some carnival," muttered Eben to himself.

"ERTADU BITSY NUSTERD HUABWD UDF IUWUS KSUBA NADR," said the driver.

"Reckon you must be some furriner," said Eben. "I don't understand you."

"RTFD HRGA BJBKUT BTSFRD KTYFTY?" said the driver.

"Can't you talk English?" said Eben curiously.

The driver got out. His spindly legs did not lift him to a height in excess of Eben's shirt pocket. He began to rummage around inside the cab of the wheelless vehicle and finally produced some tubes and coils which he assembled rapidly into some sort of instrument. This he plugged into a hole in the side of the vehicle and then aimed a sort of megaphone at Eben.

"RTDR UTDF BJYSTS JIRFTC GYTFCV HUBJYT?" said the driver.

"That's a funny-looking outfit you got there," said Eben. "But shucks, I seen a lot of radios that was better. The thing don't even play."

The driver twiddled the dials while Eben spoke and then, much mystified, left off. "BRSD TYRT RTFDAY!"

"Don't do no good," said Eben. "I can't understand a word of it."

On that the driver beamed. He tuned one dial sharply. "Then you speak elementary English," said the phone.

"Of course I do. And if you do too, why didn't you do so in the first place?"

"I think you will not be insulted if I do. But usually, you know, it is considered vulgar to talk plain English. Tell me, can't you really encipher?"

"Don't reckon I ever caught myself doing it," said Eben, amused.

The driver walked around Eben, examining him. "In our language schools, you know," said the phone, "we encipher and decipher as we speak. It is grammatically correct. But you seem to be from some very distant land where plain English is still spoken. It must be a very dull place."

"I reckon we get along," said Eben. "What you got in that thing, there?"

"The truck? Oh, some junk. I was taking it down to the city dump. What have you got in that thing?"

"Well," said Eben, "I got some brandy and I got some vegetables but they're both pretty valuable."

"Brandy? Vegetables? I don't know those two words."

Eben chuckled to himself. And this feller was accusing *him* of being ignorant! "Well, I'll show you."

He gave the fellow an apple and the driver immediately pulled a small lens of a peculiar color from his pocket and looked it all over.

"It's to eat," said Eben.

"Eat?" blinked the driver, antennae waving in alarm.

"Sure," said Eben.

More anxiously than before the driver remade his examination. "Well, there's no poison in it," he said doubtfully. And then he bit it with his puny teeth and presently smiled. "Why, that is very good indeed! RTDA HRTA—"

"Now don't start that again," said Eben.

"It's excellent," said the driver. "Do you have many of these?"

"They're pretty rare," said Eben.

"What is that in the jars?"

Eben gave him a drink of the brandy and again the driver beamed.

"How this warms one! It's marvelous! Could I buy some

from you?" And he took out a card which had holes punched in it.

"What's this?" said Eben.

"That's a labor card, of course. It shows my value. Of course as the driver of a waste wagon I don't earn very much, only forty labor units a week, but it should be sufficient—"

"What kind of junk have you got in that wagon?"

"What does that have to do with my buying some of this?" said the driver.

"Mebbe we can cook up a trade," said Eben.

To find out more about *The Crossroads* and how you can obtain your copy, go to www.goldenagestories.com.

Glossary

Glossary

STORIES FROM THE GOLDEN AGE *reflect the words and expressions used in the 1930s and 1940s, adding unique flavor and authenticity to the tales. While a character's speech may often reflect regional origins, it also can convey attitudes common in the day. So that readers can better grasp such cultural and historical terms, uncommon words or expressions of the era, the following glossary has been provided.*

---

alabaster: an almost transparent white stone, often used for making decorative objects.

banca: a boat used in the Philippines, made from a single log and furnished with an outrigger.

bime-by: by and by; eventually.

bows: the exterior of the forward end of a vessel.

bridge lamp: a traditional floor lamp having a classic design with a pleated shade that diffuses the light.

buck up: gain courage.

Chamorro: a people inhabiting the Mariana Islands; also the language of these people.

copra: the dried kernel or meat of the coconut from which coconut oil is obtained.

counsel, kept his own: kept his own thoughts and intentions secret.

culverts: tunnels that carry a stream or open drain under a road.

dementia praecox: schizophrenia.

Department of Commerce: the department of the US federal government that promotes and administers domestic and foreign commerce.

djellaba: a loose-hooded cloak of a kind traditionally worn by Arabs.

droll: amusing in a strange or quaint way.

dugout: a boat made by hollowing out a log.

G-men: government men; agents of the Federal Bureau of Investigation.

gugus: natives of the Philippines.

hafa: (Chamorro) hello.

hearkened: listened attentively; heeded.

howitzers: cannons that have comparatively short barrels, used especially for firing shells at a high angle of elevation for a short range, as for reaching a target behind cover or in a trench.

Joblike: of or like Job, the central figure in a parable (story designed to teach a religious principle or moral lesson) from the Bible. Job is a man who is blameless and honorable. He feared God and turned away from evil. Despite losing his possessions, sons and health, he does not lose his faith in God.

Kaisan Isle: one of the Mariana Islands, approximately 1,500 miles (2,414 km) southeast of the Philippines.

lettered streets: streets that are oriented east to west and use a single letter of the alphabet; for example, "A Street."

longboat: a large boat that may be launched from a sailing ship.

long house: a type of long, narrow, single-roomed building that served as a communal dwelling.

lugger: a small boat used for fishing or sailing and having two or three masts, each with a four-sided sail.

Luzon: the chief island of the Philippines.

magnesium flare: a flare made of a light, silver-white, metallic element that burns with a dazzling white light.

magneto: a small electric generator containing a permanent magnet and used to provide high-voltage current.

mestiza: a woman of mixed native and foreign ancestry.

muezzin: a man who calls Muslims to prayer from the minaret (a slender tower with a balcony) of a mosque.

parabola: a type of curve made by an object that is thrown up in the air and falls to the ground in a different place.

pitch: a line of talk designed to persuade.

plucking up: summoning up one's courage or rousing one's spirits.

potion: a drink.

protocol: the code of international courtesy governing the conduct of those in the diplomatic service or otherwise engaged in international relations. Within the State Department, the Office of the Chief of Protocol is responsible for advising the president, vice president and secretary of state on matters of national and international diplomatic protocol.

prow: the fore part of a ship or boat, sometimes used to refer to the ship itself.

put in: to enter a port or harbor, especially for shelter, repairs or provisions.

Red Plague: smallpox.

Robber Islands: a former name for the Mariana Islands, a group of islands east of the Philippines. They were so named by the Spanish explorer who discovered the islands, when the natives robbed his ships.

sandbox: a primitive sort of spittoon, consisting of a wooden box filled with sand.

sarong: garment consisting of a long piece of cloth worn wrapped around the body and tucked under the armpits.

scarf: a long, narrow covering for a table, bureau top, etc.

Scheherazade: the female narrator of *The Arabian Nights*, who during one thousand and one adventurous nights saved her life by entertaining her husband, the king, with stories.

spraddled: spread apart.

straw: something with too little substance to provide support in a crisis.

Tiger Rag: a lively tune that gained national popularity after being recorded by the Original Dixieland Jazz Band in 1917. Hundreds of recordings of the tune appeared following this and through the 1920s. With the coming of sound film, it often appeared on soundtracks of both live action movies and animated cartoons when something very energetic was wanted.

topee: a lightweight hat worn in tropical countries for protection from the sun.

trade winds: any of the nearly constant easterly winds that dominate most of the tropics and subtropics throughout the world, blowing mainly from the northeast in the Northern Hemisphere, and from the southeast in the Southern Hemisphere.

tramp: a freight vessel that does not run regularly between fixed ports, but takes a cargo wherever shippers desire.

truck with, had no: had no dealings or associations with.

varmint: an objectionable or undesirable animal, usually predatory, as a coyote or bobcat.

what for: a punishment or scolding.

witch doctor: a person who is believed to heal through magical powers.

L. Ron Hubbard
in the Golden Age
of Pulp Fiction

In writing an adventure story
a writer has to know that he is adventuring
for a lot of people who cannot.
The writer has to take them here and there
about the globe and show them
excitement and love and realism.
As long as that writer is living the part of an
adventurer when he is hammering
the keys, he is succeeding with his story.

Adventuring is a state of mind.
If you adventure through life, you have a
good chance to be a success on paper.

Adventure doesn't mean globe-trotting,
exactly, and it doesn't mean great deeds.
Adventuring is like art.
You have to live it to make it real.

— *L. Ron Hubbard*

L. Ron Hubbard
and American
Pulp Fiction

ORN March 13, 1911, L. Ron Hubbard lived a life at
least as expansive as the stories with which he enthralled
a hundred million readers through a fifty-year career.

Originally hailing from Tilden, Nebraska, he spent his
formative years in a classically rugged Montana, replete with
the cowpunchers, lawmen and desperadoes who would later
people his Wild West adventures. And lest anyone imagine
those adventures were drawn from vicarious experience, he
was not only breaking broncs at a tender age, he was also
among the few whites ever admitted into Blackfoot society
as a bona fide blood brother. While if only to round out an
otherwise rough and tumble youth, his mother was that rarity
of her time—a thoroughly educated woman—who introduced
her son to the classics of Occidental literature even before
his seventh birthday.

But as any dedicated L. Ron Hubbard reader will attest, his
world extended far beyond Montana. In point of fact, and as the
son of a United States naval officer, by the age of eighteen he
had traveled over a quarter of a million miles. Included therein
were three Pacific crossings to a then still mysterious Asia, where
he ran with the likes of Her British Majesty's agent-in-place

for North China, and the last in the line of Royal Magicians from the court of Kublai Khan. For the record, L. Ron Hubbard was also among the first Westerners to gain admittance to forbidden Tibetan monasteries below Manchuria, and his photographs of China's Great Wall long graced American geography texts.

L. Ron Hubbard, left, at Congressional Airport, Washington, DC, 1931, with members of George Washington University flying club.

Upon his return to the United States and a hasty completion of his interrupted high school education, the young Ron Hubbard entered George Washington University. There, as fans of his aerial adventures may have heard, he earned his wings as a pioneering barnstormer at the dawn of American aviation. He also earned a place in free-flight record books for the longest sustained flight above Chicago. Moreover, as a roving reporter for *Sportsman Pilot* (featuring his first professionally penned articles), he further helped inspire a generation of pilots who would take America to world airpower.

Immediately beyond his sophomore year, Ron embarked on the first of his famed ethnological expeditions, initially to then untrammeled Caribbean shores (descriptions of which would later fill a whole series of West Indies mystery-thrillers). That the Puerto Rican interior would also figure into the future of Ron Hubbard stories was likewise no accident. For in addition to cultural studies of the island, a 1932–33

LRH expedition is rightly remembered as conducting the first complete mineralogical survey of a Puerto Rico under United States jurisdiction.

There was many another adventure along this vein: As a lifetime member of the famed Explorers Club, L. Ron Hubbard charted North Pacific waters with the first shipboard radio direction finder, and so pioneered a long-range navigation system universally employed until the late twentieth century. While not to put too fine an edge on it, he also held a rare Master Mariner's license to pilot any vessel, of any tonnage in any ocean.

Yet lest we stray too far afield, there is an LRH note at this juncture in his saga, and it reads in part:

"I started out writing for the pulps, writing the best I knew, writing for every mag on the stands, slanting as well as I could."

To which one might add: His earliest submissions date from the

Capt. L. Ron Hubbard in Ketchikan, Alaska, 1940, on his Alaskan Radio Experimental Expedition, the first of three voyages conducted under the Explorers Club flag.

summer of 1934, and included tales drawn from true-to-life Asian adventures, with characters roughly modeled on British/American intelligence operatives he had known in Shanghai. His early Westerns were similarly peppered with details drawn from personal experience. Although therein lay a first hard lesson from the often cruel world of the pulps. His first Westerns were soundly rejected as lacking the authenticity of a Max Brand yarn (a particularly frustrating comment given L. Ron Hubbard's Westerns came straight from his Montana homeland, while Max Brand was a mediocre New York poet named Frederick Schiller Faust, who turned out implausible six-shooter tales from the terrace of an Italian villa).

Nevertheless, and needless to say, L. Ron Hubbard persevered and soon earned a reputation as among the most publishable names in pulp fiction, with a ninety percent placement rate of first-draft manuscripts. He was also among the most prolific, averaging between seventy and a hundred thousand words a month. Hence the rumors that L. Ron Hubbard had redesigned a typewriter for faster keyboard action and pounded out manuscripts on a continuous roll of butcher paper to save the precious seconds it took to insert a single sheet of paper into manual typewriters of the day.

That all L. Ron Hubbard stories did not run beneath said byline is yet another aspect of pulp fiction lore. That is, as publishers periodically rejected manuscripts from top-drawer authors if only to avoid paying top dollar, L. Ron Hubbard and company just as frequently replied with submissions under various pseudonyms. In Ron's case, the

A MAN OF MANY NAMES

Between 1934 and 1950, L. Ron Hubbard authored more than fifteen million words of fiction in more than two hundred classic publications. To supply his fans and editors with stories across an array of genres and pulp titles, he adopted fifteen pseudonyms in addition to his already renowned L. Ron Hubbard byline.

Winchester Remington Colt
Lt. Jonathan Daly
Capt. Charles Gordon
Capt. L. Ron Hubbard
Bernard Hubbel
Michael Keith
Rene Lafayette
Legionnaire 148
Legionnaire 14830
Ken Martin
Scott Morgan
Lt. Scott Morgan
Kurt von Rachen
Barry Randolph
Capt. Humbert Reynolds

list included: Rene Lafayette, Captain Charles Gordon, Lt. Scott Morgan and the notorious Kurt von Rachen—supposedly on the lam for a murder rap, while hammering out two-fisted prose in Argentina. The point: While L. Ron Hubbard as Ken Martin spun stories of Southeast Asian intrigue, LRH as Barry Randolph authored tales of

L. Ron Hubbard, circa 1930, at the outset of a literary career that would finally span half a century.

romance on the Western range—which, stretching between a dozen genres is how he came to stand among the two hundred elite authors providing close to a million tales through the glory days of American Pulp Fiction.

In evidence of exactly that, by 1936 L. Ron Hubbard was literally leading pulp fiction's elite as president of New York's American Fiction Guild. Members included a veritable pulp hall of fame: Lester "Doc Savage" Dent, Walter "The Shadow" Gibson, and the legendary Dashiell Hammett—to cite but a few.

Also in evidence of just where L. Ron Hubbard stood within his first two years on the American pulp circuit: By the spring of 1937, he was ensconced in Hollywood, adopting a Caribbean thriller for Columbia Pictures, remembered today as *The Secret of Treasure Island*. Comprising fifteen thirty-minute episodes, the L. Ron Hubbard screenplay led to the most profitable matinée serial in Hollywood history. In accord with Hollywood culture, he was thereafter continually called upon

The 1937 Secret of Treasure Island, *a fifteen-episode serial adapted for the screen by L. Ron Hubbard from his novel,* Murder at Pirate Castle.

to rewrite/doctor scripts—most famously for long-time friend and fellow adventurer Clark Gable.

In the interim—and herein lies another distinctive chapter of the L. Ron Hubbard story—he continually worked to open Pulp Kingdom gates to up-and-coming authors. Or, for that matter, anyone who wished to write. It was a fairly unconventional stance, as markets were already thin and competition razor sharp. But the fact remains, it was an L. Ron Hubbard hallmark that he vehemently lobbied on behalf of young authors—regularly supplying instructional articles to trade journals, guest-lecturing to short story classes at George Washington University and Harvard, and even founding his own creative writing competition. It was established in 1940, dubbed the Golden Pen, and guaranteed winners both New York representation and publication in *Argosy*.

But it was John W. Campbell Jr.'s *Astounding Science Fiction* that finally proved the most memorable LRH vehicle. While every fan of L. Ron Hubbard's galactic epics undoubtedly knows the story, it nonetheless bears repeating: By late 1938, the pulp publishing magnate of Street & Smith was determined to revamp *Astounding Science Fiction* for broader readership. In particular, senior editorial director F. Orlin Tremaine called for stories with a stronger *human element*. When acting editor John W. Campbell balked, preferring his spaceship-driven tales, Tremaine enlisted Hubbard. Hubbard, in turn, replied with the genre's first truly *character-driven* works, wherein heroes are pitted not against bug-eyed monsters but the mystery and majesty of deep space itself—and thus was launched the Golden Age of Science Fiction.

The names alone are enough to quicken the pulse of any science fiction aficionado, including LRH friend and protégé, Robert Heinlein, Isaac Asimov, A. E. van Vogt and Ray Bradbury. Moreover, when coupled with LRH stories of fantasy, we further come to what's rightly been described as the foundation of every modern tale of horror: L. Ron Hubbard's immortal *Fear*. It was rightly proclaimed by Stephen King as one of the very few works to genuinely warrant that overworked term "classic"—as in: *"This is a classic tale of creeping, surreal menace and horror. . . . This is one of the really, really good ones."*

L. Ron Hubbard, 1948, among fellow science fiction luminaries at the World Science Fiction Convention in Toronto.

To accommodate the greater body of L. Ron Hubbard fantasies, Street & Smith inaugurated *Unknown*—a classic pulp if there ever was one, and wherein readers were soon thrilling to the likes of *Typewriter in the Sky* and *Slaves of Sleep* of which Frederik Pohl would declare: *"There are bits and pieces from Ron's work that became part of the language in ways that very few other writers managed."*

And, indeed, at J. W. Campbell Jr.'s insistence, Ron was regularly drawing on themes from the Arabian Nights and so introducing readers to a world of genies, jinn, Aladdin and Sinbad—all of which, of course, continue to float through cultural mythology to this day.

At least as influential in terms of post-apocalypse stories was L. Ron Hubbard's 1940 *Final Blackout*. Generally acclaimed as the finest anti-war novel of the decade and among the ten best works of the genre ever authored—here, too, was a tale that would live on in ways few other writers imagined.

Portland, Oregon, 1943; L. Ron Hubbard, captain of the US Navy subchaser PC 815.

Hence, the later Robert Heinlein verdict: "Final Blackout *is as perfect a piece of science fiction as has ever been written.*"

Like many another who both lived and wrote American pulp adventure, the war proved a tragic end to Ron's sojourn in the pulps. He served with distinction in four theaters and was highly decorated for commanding corvettes in the North Pacific. He was also grievously wounded in combat, lost many a close friend and colleague and thus resolved to say farewell to pulp fiction and devote himself to what it had supported these many years—namely, his serious research.

But in no way was the LRH literary saga at an end, for as he wrote some thirty years later, in 1980:

"Recently there came a period when I had little to do. This was novel in a life so crammed with busy years, and I decided to amuse myself by writing a novel that was pure science fiction."

That work was *Battlefield Earth: A Saga of the Year 3000*. It was an immediate *New York Times* bestseller and, in fact, the first international science fiction blockbuster in decades. It was not, however, L. Ron Hubbard's magnum opus, as that distinction is generally reserved for his next and final work: The 1.2 million word *Mission Earth*.

> **Final Blackout**
> *is as perfect a piece of science fiction as has ever been written.*
>
> —Robert Heinlein

How he managed those 1.2 million words in just over twelve months is yet another piece of the L. Ron Hubbard legend. But the fact remains, he did indeed author a ten-volume *dekalogy* that lives in publishing history for the fact that each and every volume of the series was also a *New York Times* bestseller.

Moreover, as subsequent generations discovered L. Ron Hubbard through republished works and novelizations of his screenplays, the mere fact of his name on a cover signaled an international bestseller. . . . Until, to date, sales of his works exceed hundreds of millions, and he otherwise remains among the most enduring and widely read authors in literary history. Although as a final word on the tales of L. Ron Hubbard, perhaps it's enough to simply reiterate what editors told readers in the glory days of American Pulp Fiction:

He writes the way he does, brothers, because he's been there, seen it and done it!

THE STORIES FROM THE GOLDEN AGE

Your ticket to adventure starts here with the Stories from the Golden Age collection by master storyteller L. Ron Hubbard. These gripping tales are set in a kaleidoscope of exotic locales and brim with fascinating characters, including some of the most vile villains, dangerous dames and brazen heroes you'll ever get to meet.

The entire collection of over one hundred and fifty stories is being released in a series of eighty books and audiobooks. For an up-to-date listing of available titles, go to www.goldenagestories.com.

AIR ADVENTURE

117

FAR-FLUNG ADVENTURE

SEA ADVENTURE

TALES FROM THE ORIENT

The Devil—With Wings
The Falcon Killer
Five Mex for a Million
Golden Hell
The Green God
Hurricane's Roar
Inky Odds
Orders Is Orders

Pearl Pirate
The Red Dragon
Spy Killer
Tah
The Trail of the Red Diamonds
Wind-Gone-Mad
Yellow Loot

MYSTERY

The Blow Torch Murder
Brass Keys to Murder
Calling Squad Cars!
The Carnival of Death
The Chee-Chalker
Dead Men Kill
The Death Flyer
Flame City

The Grease Spot
Killer Ape
Killer's Law
The Mad Dog Murder
Mouthpiece
Murder Afloat
The Slickers
They Killed Him Dead

119

FANTASY

Borrowed Glory *If I Were You*
The Crossroads *The Last Drop*
Danger in the Dark *The Room*
The Devil's Rescue *The Tramp*
He Didn't Like Cats

SCIENCE FICTION

The Automagic Horse *A Matter of Matter*
Battle of Wizards *The Obsolete Weapon*
Battling Bolto *One Was Stubborn*
The Beast *The Planet Makers*
Beyond All Weapons *The Professor Was a Thief*
A Can of Vacuum *The Slaver*
The Conroy Diary *Space Can*
The Dangerous Dimension *Strain*
Final Enemy *Tough Old Man*
The Great Secret *240,000 Miles Straight Up*
Greed *When Shadows Fall*
The Invaders

120

WESTERN

Discover Fantastic Worlds
at a Strange Crossroads in Time!

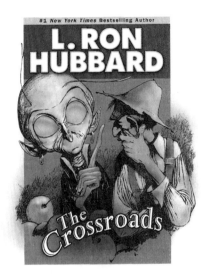

Frustrated with a government that pays him to bury surplus produce in order to "fix" the economy while city folk starve, farmer Eben Smith decides to take matters into his own hands. He piles up his wagon with ripe fruits and vegetables and sets out for the first time to barter his goods in the big city.

Being Eben's first city trip and all, the way soon becomes uncertain. But when Eben comes across a strange crossroads, he discovers that he's fallen into a nexus in time. Soon he's bartering a lot more than goods with different cultures in alternative realities . . . accidentally wreaking havoc and chaos in each.

Get
The Crossroads

PAPERBACK OR AUDIOBOOK: $9.95 EACH
Free Shipping & Handling for Book Club Members
CALL TOLL-FREE: 1-877-8GALAXY (1-877-842-5299)
OR GO ONLINE TO **www.goldenagestories.com**

Galaxy Press, 7051 Hollywood Blvd., Suite 200, Hollywood, CA 90028

JOIN THE PULP REVIVAL
America in the 1930s and 40s

Pulp fiction was in its heyday and 30 million readers were regularly riveted by the larger-than-life tales of master storyteller L. Ron Hubbard. For this was pulp fiction's golden age, when the writing was raw and every page packed a walloping punch.

That magic can now be yours. An evocative world of nefarious villains, exotic intrigues, courageous heroes and heroines—a world that today's cinema has barely tapped for tales of adventure and swashbucklers.

Enroll today in the Stories from the Golden Age Club and begin receiving your monthly feature edition selected from more than 150 stories in the collection.

You may choose to enjoy them as either a paperback or audiobook for the special membership price of $9.95 each month along with FREE shipping and handling.

CALL TOLL-FREE: 1-877-8GALAXY
(1-877-842-5299) OR GO ONLINE TO
www.goldenagestories.com
AND BECOME PART OF THE PULP REVIVAL!

Prices are set in US dollars only. For non-US residents, please call
1-323-466-7815 for pricing information. Free shipping available for US residents only.

Galaxy Press, 7051 Hollywood Blvd., Suite 200, Hollywood, CA 90028